PRAISE FOR *GIRL, STOLEN*

An ALA Best Book for Young Adults

An ALA Quick Pick for Young Adults

A Barnes & Noble Top Teen Pick

Winner of the Maryland Black-Eyed Susan Book Award

A Missouri Truman Readers Award Selection

"Constantly interesting and suspenseful." —*Kirkus Reviews*

PRAISE FOR *THE NIGHT SHE DISAPPEARED*

An ALA Top Ten Quick Pick for Young Adults

A TLA Tayshas Selection

A Junior Library Guild Selection

"[A] fast-paced, gripping thriller." —*School Library Journal*

PRAISE FOR *THE GIRL WHO WAS SUPPOSED TO DIE*

"Shrewd characterizations lend additional substance to this adrenaline-inducing read." —*Publishers Weekly*

"Henry has turned up the intensity . . . with this edge-of-your-seat thriller." —*School Library Journal*

PRAISE FOR THE POINT LAST SEEN SERIES

"Henry has become a leading light in YA mystery." —*Booklist*

★"Fast paced and fascinating." —*VOYA*, starred review

"The author's expertise at plotting a murder mystery and knowledge of police procedure are evident."
—*Publishers Weekly*

OTHER MYSTERIES BY APRIL HENRY:

Girl, Stolen

The Night She Disappeared

The Girl Who Was Supposed to Die

Count All Her Bones

THE POINT LAST SEEN SERIES

The Body in the Woods

Blood Will Tell

THE GIRL
I USED
TO BE

THE GIRL
I USED
TO BE

APRIL HENRY

SQUARE
FISH

Christy Ottaviano Books

HENRY HOLT AND COMPANY • NEW YORK

SQUARE
FISH

An imprint of Macmillan Publishing Group, LLC
175 Fifth Avenue
New York, NY 10010
fiercereads.com

Square Fish and the Square Fish logo are trademarks of Macmillan and
are used by Henry Holt and Company under license from Macmillan.

Our books may be purchased in bulk for promotional, educational, or business
use. Please contact your local bookseller or the Macmillan Corporate and
Premium Sales Department at (800) 221-7945 ext. 5442 or by e-mail
at MacmillanSpecialMarkets@macmillan.com.

Library of Congress Cataloging-in-Publication Data
Names: Henry, April, author.
Title: The girl I used to be / April Henry.
Description: New York : Henry Holt and Company, 2016. | Summary:
"Olivia's parents were killed fourteen years ago. Now, new evidence
reopens the case . . . and she finds herself involved" —Provided by
publisher.
Identifiers: LCCN 2015026176 | ISBN 978-1-250-11523-2 (paperback) |
ISBN 978-1-62779-333-9 (ebook)
Subjects: | CYAC: Mystery and detective stories. | Murder—Fiction. |
Identity—Fiction. | Parents—Fiction. | Orphans—Fiction. |
BISAC: JUVENILE FICTION / Mysteries & Detective Stories. |
JUVENILE FICTION / Family / Orphans & Foster Homes.
Classification: LCC PZ7.H39356 Gi 2016 | DDC [Fic]—dc23
LC record available at http://lccn.loc.gov/2015026176

Originally published in the United States by Christy Ottaviano Books/
Henry Holt and Company
First Square Fish edition: 2017
Square Fish logo designed by Filomena Tuosto

7   9   10   8

This book is for my mom, who always said I would write my best book because of grief. I read the first few chapters to her when she was in hospice. For many years, my mom was the only person who read what I wrote. I am still striving to be the woman she was: kind, spontaneous, funny, and helpful.

CHAPTER 1

SCATTER MY BONES

THE ONLY SOUND I CAN HEAR IS MY OWN panicked breathing. I'm running flat out through the forest. Then my toe catches a root, and suddenly I'm flying.

Until I'm not. I come down hard. With my hands cuffed in front of me, I can't even really break my fall. Despite the plastic boot on my left leg, I'm up again in a crazy scrambling second, spitting out dirt and pine needles as I start sprinting again.

Running like my life depends on it. Because it does.

Three weeks ago, I was living in Portland. Working in a supermarket deli. Slicing turkey breast and handing out cheese samples on toothpicks.

Now I'm hurtling through the Southern Oregon woods, being chased by a killer. And no one knows I'm here.

Because of the handcuffs, I can't pump my fists. Instead, I have to swing them in tandem. Trying to avoid another fall, I lift my knees higher as the ground rises. I can't hear my pursuer, just my own panting breath.

If I don't come back, will Duncan ever know what happened to me? These woods can hide things for years. Will animals scatter my bones, plants twine around my remains?

When I reach the top of the hill, I don't slow down. Instead, I try to lengthen my stride. It's impossible to maintain a rhythm. I leap over a log, splash through the silver thread of a creek. My mouth is so dry. It tastes of dirt and the bitterness of fear.

A Steller's jay startles up from a branch, squawking. If only I could take wing and fly. But I'm stuck here on earth, legs churning, staggering over this uneven ground.

I can't stop or I'll die.

The reality is that I'm probably going to die anyway. And if that's so, I'm going to go down fighting.

THE KALEIDOSCOPE SHIFTS

IT BEGINS WITH A NAME I HAVEN'T HEARD IN years. Except in my dreams.

"Ariel? Ariel Benson?"

I freeze.

Ten seconds ago, someone knocked on my apartment door. Through the peephole, I saw two men, one with a white band for a collar. I didn't feel like talking to missionaries, with their brochures printed on limp paper, so I turned away.

But then they said my name. My old name.

Now I open the door a few inches. They're in their midthirties. About the right age to be my dad. A bubble expands in my chest.

"Ariel Benson?" the man in the rumpled suit repeats, his pale eyes locking onto mine. Nothing about him is familiar.

I nod. When I try to swallow, my tongue is a piece of leather.

"I'm Detective Campbell. And this is Chaplain Farben.

We're with the Portland police, but we're here on behalf of the Medford police." Medford is more than four hours away. It's where I was born. "Can we come in?"

Cops. The kaleidoscope shifts. Should I be disappointed—or relieved? I step back, feeling embarrassed by the open box of Lucky Charms on the scarred coffee table.

They take the blue futon couch. I sit on the green striped chair I found on the side of the road two months ago. Since they're cops, I know what they must be here to tell me. And it's not that one of them is my father. "So you found my dad?"

All these years, I've imagined where he might have run to. Mexico? Cambodia? Venezuela? Some place where he could forget what he did. But the law must have finally caught up with him.

The detective's brow furrows. "Has someone been in contact with you?"

I've made sure no one knows the truth about who I am. Who I come from. "Just guessing." I shrug, like I don't care. "Why else would two cops be here?"

"Is there someone you would want us to call, Ariel?" the chaplain asks. He has a round, pale face, like the moon. "Someone you'd like to have with you?"

I wish they would just cut to the chase. "I'm an emancipated minor." I don't need an adult here. According to the law, I *am* an adult, even though I only just turned seventeen. "So where did you find him?"

The detective pulls out a notebook and flips to the top page. "It was actually a woman walking her dog. In the

4

woods about a mile from where your mother's body was found."

At first, I imagine my dad as some crazy, long-haired guy living off the grid, but then I realize they're not talking about him living in a cabin. The pieces shift and fall again.

They're talking about a body.

The world slows down. "You mean he's dead? My father's dead?"

Startled, the two men exchange a glance.

I press my hand to my mouth, lifting it long enough to say, "Can you start from the beginning, please?"

The detective sucks in a breath. "You're Ariel Benson, right?"

It's simpler just to agree. "Right." The adoption eight years ago didn't work out, but I kept the name. Olivia Reinhart. I left Ariel Benson behind.

"And your mother was Naomi Benson. And your father was Terry Weeks." The detective watches me carefully. "Is that right?"

I nod, still trying to get used to the repetition of the word *was*.

"Nearly fourteen years ago, your mother's body was found in the forest in Southern Oregon."

"Right. My dad killed her and then drove up here. Along the way, he dropped me off at the Salem Walmart. He parked at the airport and then took off." Wiped his truck clean, left it in the long-term lot, and vanished. This was before September 11, when it was a lot easier to just fly away without leaving a record of where you went. Leaving behind your murdered girlfriend and your three-year-old daughter. "So I don't understand. How could his body be in the forest?"

"Not his whole body," the detective corrects me. "So far, all the Medford police have is his jawbone. It was found about a month ago, but there weren't enough teeth left to match dental records. They just got the DNA results back."

Even though I'm sitting down, the floor feels far away.

The chaplain leans forward. "Ariel, what you said was the working theory the Medford police have had all these years. But the discovery of your father's remains changes that. They now think he was murdered, probably at the same time as your mother, and by the same person."

I try to take it in. My father's not a killer. He's not in some foreign country. He's not going to show up at my door to see how I turned out.

He's been dead for nearly fourteen years.

I snatch at one of the dozens of thoughts whirling through my brain. "But you said it"—I'm not going to say *jawbone*, I'm *not*—"was a mile from where my mom was found. Why weren't they found together?"

The detective shrugs. "It's hard to know. Your mother's body wasn't found for, what"—he looks down at his notebook and back up at me—"three weeks? Animal predation could have disturbed the remains. The killer could have moved one of the bodies. Maybe one of your parents tried to run. The Medford police don't even know how your father was killed, because they only have the jawbone."

All my life, I've known what I am. The daughter of

a victim and a killer. When I looked in the mirror, sometimes I thought I could see them both—the cowering and the rage.

Part of my dad was in me, and that meant I could grow up to be like him. Every time I lost my temper, I felt it pulse deep inside. The knowledge that I could do something as crazy as he did, stab someone I was supposed to love and leave them with only the cold stars as witnesses.

But now what am I? What was my father?

And there's something else.

If my dad didn't kill my mom, if his body has always been in the forest—then who drove me to the Walmart three hours away?

I imagine the three-year-old me. I've thought about that girl so much, what she might have seen, what she knew, what it was like being in that truck with her dad after he killed her mother.

I don't remember ever being that girl. Not what happened that day or before. Is not remembering a gift or a curse?

And now everything has been turned on its head.

"Too bad you were too young to remember anything." The detective meets my eyes. His own are a washed blue. "Although that's probably what saved you. Because the Medford police believe it must have been your parents' killer who took you to the Walmart."

CHAPTER 3

TWISTED LOVE

THE ROOM IS SPINNING. I CLOSE MY EYES. When everyone thought my dad had killed my mom, it made sense that he hadn't killed me. I was his daughter, his own blood.

"But why not?" I manage to ask. "If the killer had already murdered my parents, why didn't he kill me?"

The detective straightens up. "You just said 'he.'" He and the chaplain watch me closely.

"Yeah? So?"

"Does that mean you remember that the killer was a man? The police down in Medford want to know if you have any memories of what happened. Especially in light of this new evidence."

"I don't remember anything. It just seems likely it was a man, that's all. What woman would stab another woman nineteen times?" I can't imagine even stabbing someone once. In biology class last year, we had to cut an earthworm in half and then sew it back together. I'll never forget the way the worm's skin resisted and finally gave way with a pop.

Detective Campbell shrugs. "You'd be surprised. It could have been a woman. Maybe not a stranger, not that many times, but a woman who knew your mom and hated her. Or who panicked and felt like she had to make sure your mom was dead." The chaplain pulls a face at the bluntness, but the detective doesn't stop. "You're right, though. In cases like this, it's more than likely a male perpetrator. As to why he—or maybe she—didn't kill you, he probably figured you were too young to say what you had seen. Or he knew you, and that held him back. Or he felt wrong killing a child. Some killers target specific victims but would never hurt someone who doesn't meet that profile."

"Could it have been a stranger?" I ask. "Some crazy guy they just met in the woods?"

"There are two reasons to kill someone you don't know," Detective Campbell says. "The primary one is because they have something you want, and you do what you need to do to take it from them. Even murder." His voice is matter-of-fact.

I can't imagine being that cold. "So someone might have killed my parents so they could steal from them?"

"But there's one problem with that scenario. What would they have stolen?" He lifts his empty hands. "From what the Medford police told us, your parents didn't have much money. And the killer didn't do it for your dad's truck, because it was left at the airport. And they didn't do it for you, because they left you at the Walmart. So stealing as a motive doesn't seem likely."

I nod, my thoughts still spinning.

"But some people kill because they like killing. And in those cases, the murder isn't something that just happens. It's what you want in the first place. It's what you live for."

The way he says *you* creeps me out, as if he thinks any of us could be a person with twisted desires.

"Was my mom alive the whole time?" I've wondered that for years.

"There was some decomposition"—Chaplain Farben clears his throat as if warning Detective Campbell not to get too graphic, but he continues—"so they couldn't say for sure. She could have been dead for some of it. They do know she fought back. Some of those wounds were defensive cuts to her forearms and hands." He raises his hands over his head as if trying to shield himself. "And who knows? There's nothing to say the killer didn't stab your father to death, too. We don't have enough of his body to know."

His answer just raises another question. "Then why didn't animals get my mom?"

"The killer wrapped her in a tarp."

I shiver. "Why would they do that?"

"It's not uncommon for the killer to cover the victim afterward. They feel guilty about what they've done. That's one reason the Medford police thought your dad did it. That and the overkill."

"Overkill?"

"If your goal is to kill someone, you don't need to stab them so many times. Nineteen times tells me there was some type of passion involved. Either extreme anger or someone who loved to kill or who felt some kind of twisted love for your mom. The Medford police weren't wrong to think it was your dad. The first person I would have looked at would be a boyfriend or a husband. A lover."

I shiver. It's crazy to think someone you once loved, who once loved you, could stab you and stab you and keep stabbing you. Even after you were dead.

CHAPTER 4

UNSOLVED MYSTERIES

THE COPS FINALLY LEAVE.

I don't have any pictures of my parents. When you're in the system, you don't have much that's yours. Instead of a suitcase, it's a garbage bag or a cardboard box. Every time you get taken to a new place, things get lost or stolen.

But I know where I can see my mom and dad.

I open my laptop and go to YouTube. Nearly fourteen years ago, my family was featured three times on *America's Most Wanted*. Since then, people have sliced and diced the old shows and put the segments on YouTube. Sometimes it's just an off-center video by someone who filmed their TV set.

The first is from about a week after my family went missing. I've seen the host, John Walsh, on TV. Now he has gray hair, but in this video, it's shiny black. Looking serious, he talks fast.

"Southern Oregon's Cascade Range is a place where people go to get away from it all. This peaceful mountain setting is also the last known destination for a missing family who went looking for a Christmas tree and never came back."

When this episode aired, I had already been found and was in foster care. No one realized that a missing family was related to one little girl found three hours away, one who answered questions with a blank stare.

"On December sixth," Walsh says, "Terry Weeks and Naomi Benson told friends they planned to take their three-year-old daughter, Ariel, to look for a Christmas tree. They have not been seen since, and it's unknown if they even made it to their planned destination. Their vehicle has not been located by Forest Service personnel or by a helicopter Terry Weeks's father hired."

Next on-screen is Jack Weeks. My grandfather. When I was eleven, my caseworker told me he had died. Since I didn't have any memories of him, it didn't mean much. He may have loved his son enough to hire a helicopter, but that love hadn't extended to giving me a home when I was all alone.

On YouTube he looks rugged and tanned, like he'll live forever. He says, "If they made it to the woods, why haven't we found Terry's truck? Terry's an experienced outdoorsman. He and Naomi have a child with them. They wouldn't have gone far from a road. Something must have happened before they even got there."

The camera cuts back to Walsh in the studio. "Terry Weeks is twenty-one. Naomi Benson is twenty. And little Ariel Benson is just three. Look closely at their photos and that of this Dodge truck, which is similar to the truck Terry Weeks drove."

The screen shows an orange pickup with the license plate blurred out. And then there's a photo of the three of us.

I hit Pause. We are at the beach, on what must have been one of those rare warm days at the Oregon coast. I'm on my mom's lap. I don't remember being blond, but I used to be. My mom's wavy brown hair falls past her shoulders. She has high cheekbones, dark eyebrows, and eyes that slant down at the corners. If my computer was a mirror, I'd see something similar, only my nose doesn't turn up. It's long and straight, like my dad's, and I have his strong chin.

My dad's dark blond hair is a little too long. Shirtless, he sits on the blanket next to my mom, with one arm slung around her waist. The fingers of his other hand curl around my small shoulder.

When I first found this photo online, it made me shudder. My father's hands looked possessive, like he could dictate anything, including whether we lived or died.

The photo hasn't changed, but I have. My chest hurts.

Now I see nothing but love, or an attempt at love, in the way he touches us. He was trying to do the right things: act like a family, pose for a vacation photo, search for a Christmas tree in a forest. I don't know if he did it for me, my mom, or himself, but still, he tried. I do know he was raised by his dad after his mom died, just like my mom was raised by her mom after her parents divorced. Neither of them really knowing how to make a whole family.

I look at their faces and wonder: Did one of them have to watch the other die? My head fills with water.

I click to resume the clip. Walsh says, "Family members say it's totally out of character for Weeks and Benson to just disappear. So please, if you know anything, call 1-800-CRIMETV."

A day after the show aired, the foster mom took me to a doctor for a scratch on my face that had become infected. The nurse thought I looked familiar. The police asked my grandmother to drive up, and she identified me.

Which is about the point where the second *America's Most Wanted* picks up.

Walsh says, "When we showed you the photo of Terry Weeks, Naomi Benson, and their daughter, Ariel, you helped us locate the missing little girl. She was found at a Walmart three hours north of where authorities were looking for her family. Little Ariel was hungry and dirty, and her face was scratched. And her parents were nowhere to be found." He raises his eyebrows. "For now, Ariel is living with her grandmother."

The camera cuts away to a face I do remember: Grandma. Wearing a purple sweatshirt, she says to the camera, "When I walked into the room, Ariel held her arms out and said 'Grandma' and ran to me. I've had her ever since."

"Ever since" turned out to be four years. Then Grandma had a heart attack and died. And I went back into foster care, more or less for good.

"Ariel used to be such a lively little thing, but now she doesn't seem happy." Grandma's fingers twist together. "We've tried asking her where Naomi and Terry are, but all she's ever said is, 'Mommy's dancing.'"

On the screen, a three-year-old me holds out a stuffed

purple frog to a framed photo of my mom. Grandma tells Walsh that I like to share things with my mom.

Although I don't remember being filmed, sometimes I think maybe I do have some memories of my parents. I don't know if they're real. They've been handled and stretched and frayed until now; they're memories of memories of memories. A man peeling me an apple. And my mother brushing my hair while we watched *SpongeBob SquarePants*. At least I think it was her. Just the sensation of it. So soothing. Feeling loved and safe and cared for.

I haven't felt like that since Grandma died.

On my computer, Grandma sighs. "I think Ariel knows something. She's withdrawn. Her personality definitely isn't the same."

The final episode was filmed after my mom's body was found, three weeks after my parents disappeared. There are quick shots of snowy woods, sniffing bloodhounds, a man waving a metal detector over the snow. Walsh speaks as the screen cuts to men carrying a long, black-wrapped bundle to an ambulance waiting with its lights off.

"This week, some of the questions surrounding the little girl mysteriously abandoned at a Walmart were tragically answered when grouse hunters found the body of her mother, Naomi Benson, in the Oregon forest. She had been stabbed to death. Terry Weeks and his truck have not been located. While there are rumors the two had a rocky relationship, for now Naomi's death and Terry's disappearance remain a mystery, a secret held close by the wilderness. Once again, America, we need your help."

It would be several more weeks before my dad's truck

was found hundreds of miles away, in the Portland airport's long-term parking lot.

Walsh's voice is a mix of optimism and determination. "There's not much to go on, but together we can solve this case. The crucial time is December sixth. If you were in the southern Oregon Cascades that day, or at the Salem Walmart, or if you saw any of these people or this truck, the police need to know. Naomi Benson deserves justice. You could be the one to bring it to her."

But it wasn't just my mother who needed justice. My dad did, too. Someone murdered both of them and left their families to wonder and worry. In my dad's case, for years.

I uncurl my fists. My fingernails have left red half-moons in my palms.

On the *Medford Mail Tribune* website, I skim the main story, headlined "Formerly Thought Killer, Man Now Considered Victim."

. . . Medford Chief of Police Stephen Spaulding said, "I remember that case well. I was a search-and-rescue volunteer, and after Naomi was found, we searched those woods for evidence, but we didn't find anything useful." He added that he hoped the discovery of Terry Weeks's remains will help jump-start the case, although the passage of time and the lack of evidence might make it difficult to solve.

What about evidence in people's memories, the way Walsh talked about? Someone has to know—or have guessed—what happened that day.

"For the past fourteen years, a cloud has hung over my brother," said Terry Weeks's sister, Carly Weeks-Tailor. "I know everyone thought that Terry was a killer, that he was living in another country, that he just abandoned his daughter. I wish our dad were alive to know the truth."

Weeks's sister said a service is planned for 2 PM on Saturday at the Perl Funeral Home, and she urges anyone with memories or photos of Weeks to bring them to share. "At least now we can finally grieve," she said.

I don't have to work on Saturday. I could drive down.

But it would be stupid to go. It's not like my dad will be there. Chances are, even his jawbone won't be. It's probably still police property.

CHAPTER 5

JUST TRYING TO GET HOME

"REGULAR FILL, PLEASE," I TELL THE GAS
station guy. How much is it going to cost to drive there
and back, plus get a hotel? Maybe I'll just come home after
the funeral. If I get too tired, I can lock my doors and
sleep in a rest area.

In the backseat is a duffel bag with my laptop, a book,
and a few clothes. Not much, but it nearly cleaned out my
closet. What do you wear to a funeral? In the movies, it's
a black dress, stockings, pumps. Sometimes a hat with a
veil. I don't have a black dress or a fancy hat. I brought
a pair of black work pants and a plain black T-shirt, and
they'll have to do.

I can't remember if I went to my mom's funeral or
what I wore to my grandmother's. I was seven when
Grandma died, old enough to know she was in the long
wooden box. Too old to hide underneath a pew, crying,
but that's what I did. People stood in the back, arguing. About me. I put my hands over my ears, but I still

saw lips curl back, heard the hiss of words, saw fingers point in my direction.

Huddled miserably underneath that pew, I knew what the arguing was about. No one wanted me. Me with my nightmares and my bad parents, one dead and one on the run.

The gas guy interrupts my thoughts with a total that makes me flinch. After I leave, I try not to hear the squeal that happens when I make a sharp right turn. My Mazda 323 is three years older than I am. The color is "champagne beige," but it's really just tan. I got the car off Craigslist. Since I can't afford to fix anything, I keep the stereo turned up and pretend I don't hear bad noises. I get on the freeway and start heading south.

After Grandma died, I was in foster care, first with one family and then another. They've all blurred together. Was the first family the one with three dogs? The one with four sets of bunk beds? The one where the parents got a divorce?

Then when I was eight, I was told I was getting a forever family.

Only it wasn't really a family. Just a woman, Tamsin Reinhart, who had visited a few times. She was an orthopedic surgeon in Portland. She was in her forties and had never been married. Maybe at some point she could have had a baby of her own, but Tamsin was all about efficiency. Adopting an older kid meant she could skip diapers and toilet training and the terrible twos. An eight-year-old, she must have figured, already knew how to dress herself and entertain herself and do pretty much what she was told. Tamsin—she wanted me to call her Mom, but I never did—bought us matching mother-daughter dresses to wear to church the first Sunday after the adoption. Pale green with little yellow flowers, the dresses swirled around our ankles when we walked. She held my hand, even though I tried to pull away, and afterward everyone came up to compliment us.

But I missed Medford. I missed my friends. I missed my school. I still missed my grandmother, with her soft body and unrestrained laugh. Every Halloween she dressed like a witch, ratted up her hair, and took out her top teeth. Tamsin was stiff and careful and never less than perfectly dressed. I had nightmares nearly every night— I still have them—and Tamsin didn't know how to deal with my screaming as I fought off invisible monsters.

And I missed my name. My real name. Ariel Benson. When she adopted me, Tamsin had it changed to Olivia Reinhart. *Reinhart* so we would have the same last name, like a real mother and daughter. And *Olivia* because she thought Ariel sounded tacky, like the mermaid in the Disney movie.

It's true. I remember Grandma talking about it. My mom named me after a cartoon movie character.

At Tamsin's, I was lonely and scared, but determined not to show it. And I was angry, too, at all the changes everyone said were for my benefit. Looking back, I don't think anyone prepared Tamsin for how I would test her. That first week, she gave me a book she'd loved when she was a girl, *Black Beauty*, and I "accidentally" spilled water on it. I spit out the tasteless pale yellow macaroni and cheese she made. I'd never had homemade before. And every day, I told her I wanted to go back to my old foster family, where there weren't any rules about bedtime or watching TV or not eating before dinner.

I didn't trust that it was real. So I pushed Tamsin away. And it worked.

Within three months, I was back in the foster system. Tamsin cried when the grim-faced social worker drove up to the house, but still, she let me go. When I was younger, I told myself that it was proof she hadn't really loved me. Maybe the truth was it could have worked out if both of us hadn't been so hurt or if we had given it more time.

I thought if Tamsin gave me back, I could return to my old life. But I didn't get anything back, not even my old name. The social worker said it would be too confusing to change, since they had decided I should stay in the same Portland school Tamsin had enrolled me in.

The freeway sign reads SALEM NEXT 3 EXITS. An hour has slipped by. It's only nine, and the funeral's not until two. I haven't been back to the Salem Walmart since I was found there nearly fourteen years ago. Maybe going in will help me remember what happened.

Inside, it's crammed with people and TVs, shoes and ketchup, toilet paper and tubs of blue cotton candy. I was found curled up underneath a fake Christmas tree, but since it's August, the seasonal display's theme is back-to-school. The crayons and pink erasers feel full of promise. Every time I started at a new school, I told myself things would be different. This time I would have tons of friends. This time I would raise my hand. This time math would make sense.

This Walmart just seems exactly like the Portland

Walmart I've been to a half dozen times. I get down on one knee, like I'm going to tie one of my black Vans, but really it's so I'm about the same height as a little kid. I squint. Does any of it feel familiar? The shelves looming overhead, the bright lights?

And there's a worker in this row now, a middle-aged guy in a red vest, filling a display with packages of yellow pencils but looking at me. Does he think I'm a shoplifter?

I guess my missing memories won't be restored like a puzzle piece snapping into place. I walk out empty-handed and get back in the car.

The farther south I go, the bluer the sky gets. The clouds thin and disappear. The day heats up, so I roll down my window. I drive through long miles of evergreens, forests that stretch to the horizon.

I find a radio station playing old music from the nineties. In a couple of years, I'll be as old as my parents were when they died. It's as if they're stuck in amber, like the scorpion in a necklace I once saw at Goodwill. They'll forever be wearing out-of-date clothes and smiling with slightly crooked teeth they couldn't afford to get fixed.

I've got those same teeth. Foster care doesn't pay for braces.

At the rest area outside Roseburg, a dark-haired girl sits cross-legged in front of the cinder-block restroom, her head tipped back against the wall, her eyes closed. Her sign reads JUST TRYING TO GET HOME. As I leave, I put a dollar bill in her white paper cup, but she doesn't stir.

Finally, I'm through the mountains and driving down into the Rogue River valley. It's more a feeling than a memory, but these tawny, folded hills, like a golden blanket pushed down to the foot of a giant's bed, are so familiar.

It's only four miles to Medford, and I've still got nearly two hours before the funeral. There's one other place I want to go.

My grandmother's house. My house, really, or it will be when I turn eighteen. Until then, I get the rental income. At least I used to, until three months ago, when the last tenant left.

I take the exit and follow the directions. And there's the house, familiar and not. Tiny and square, gray, with peeling white shutters that were probably last painted long before Grandma died.

I park next to a huge yucca bush with sword-shaped leaves. A sign stuck in the tall grass reads FOR RENT BY LEE REALTY.

I'm looking through the front window at a worn gold couch next to a battered coffee table, when I hear a voice behind me.

"I know who you must be."

CHAPTER 6

SEEING DOUBLE

I WHIRL AROUND, MY HEART A BIRD IN A TOO-small cage.

An old lady stands smiling with crowded teeth traced with gold. A rivulet of sweat is tracing its way down my spine, but she wears black corduroy pants, a crisp blue shirt with white stripes, and a black cardigan. Buttoned.

"So who am I?" I say lightly, as if the answer doesn't matter.

"You're the new renter, right? I'm glad they finally got someone in the house." Her high cheekbones are as red as apples, but the rest of her face is pale.

Suddenly, I feel as if I'm seeing double. It's like that drawing of a vase, the one where if you look at it right, it changes to two people facing each other. I see an old lady dressed in black, but my memory superimposes another image.

I see: silver hair cut to her chin.

I remember: dark, silver-streaked hair worn in a braid that fell past her shoulders.

I see: red-framed glasses.

I remember: gold wire frames.

I see: eyes caught in a net of wrinkles.

I remember: those same golden-brown eyes, but in a fuller face.

Seeing the new and the old, the real and the memory, makes me dizzy. I steady myself against the peeling gray siding.

Her face creased with concern, she touches my wrist lightly. My memory offers me her arms, pulling me close into the soft smell of baby powder.

"Honey, are you all right?" Her voice is a little too loud, like she's slightly deaf.

I manage to nod. "It's probably just the heat."

"I wish I could get warm." Her fingers twist against each other. "My heart doesn't work too well."

My own heart is still racing. "So you're the neighbor?"

"That's right. Nora Murdoch." She offers me her hand, cool skin over bones as delicate as a bird's wing.

Nora Murdoch was our neighbor and Grandma's best friend. They would sit in the living room and drink cup after cup of coffee. Every Christmas, Nora would bake gingerbread men and let me help decorate them. She didn't mind if the frosting came out in big globs or if I used too many sprinkles.

Nora is the one I ran to that terrible day when I came home from school and found my grandmother on the kitchen floor. Grandma was lying in a puddle of cold coffee, surrounded by the blue-and-white shards of what had been her favorite cup. Her skin was cold, her open eyes dull.

"I'm Olivia Reinhart."

But there's no answering spark in her eyes. I'm sure she remembers—maybe even still loves—seven-year-old blond Ariel Benson. But I'm not her. Now I'm seventeen-year-old brown-haired Olivia Reinhart. If I tell her who I am, she'll have all kinds of questions. And then she'll tell someone else, and pretty soon every eye will be on me. It's better to keep my distance. I don't want to be the center of attention, of whispers and questions. My plan is to slip in and out without being noticed.

Ten years ago, I was just a kid, but I can tell that Nora is basically the same person she was then. Just older.

Underscoring that idea, she says. "I have lived in this neighborhood forever, so if there's anything you want to know, just ask."

"Um, I'm not actually sure I'm going to rent this house. I'm still thinking about it."

"The murders didn't happen here, if that's what you're worried about," Nora says.

"Murders?"

She stamps one of her black knockoff Keds, mouth twisting with annoyance. "Oh, now you've gone and done it, Nora Murdoch. You and your big mouth! If there's one thing a potential renter doesn't want to hear, it's the word 'murder.'" Her eyes flash up to mine. "You need to know that nothing bad happened in this house, Olivia. Ever. This house has nothing but good memories."

"Then why did you say 'murders'?" I'm sweating all over now. Even the bottoms of my feet feel slick.

"Is it okay if we sit down?" Nora is already lowering herself to the steps, which are shaded by a tall oak tree. "I'm feeling a little light-headed myself today."

I sit next to her, glad to have something between me and the white ball of the sun.

"The story's been all over the news," she says. "That's why I thought you knew. My friend Sharon used to live in this house with her daughter, Naomi, and Naomi's little girl, Ariel. But almost fourteen years ago, Naomi and her boyfriend, Terry, went out with Ariel to get a Christmas tree and never came back. Someone killed Naomi in the woods. Not here."

I try to think of how a stranger might react. "Oh my God. That's terrible. Who killed her?"

"Naomi and Terry fought sometimes. For years, everyone thought Terry must have snapped and killed her and then just took off. But now his jawbone has been found in the woods. And the police think both of them were murdered by someone else." In a near whisper, Nora adds, "And I spent all those years thinking he did it."

I understand far better than she can imagine. "But you said everyone thought that. Not just you."

"I was too quick to judge." She sighs. "Anyway, Naomi dying just about broke Sharon's heart. In fact, she died of a heart attack a few years later. I'm sure it was losing her daughter that did it." She falls silent. Her lower lip trembles. "I'm the one who's supposed to have a bad heart. Never thought I'd still be here all these years later."

Will Nora put two and two together if I ask about myself? Then again, if I don't, I might seem cold. "What happened to the little girl? Your friend's granddaughter? Was she killed, too?"

"She was found three hours away. After the police figured out who she was, Ariel ended up back with Sharon. She was too young to say what had happened. We asked her and asked her. All she would say was 'Mommy's dancing.' After Sharon died, Ariel went into foster care. I heard she got adopted up in Portland. I tried to take her in, but the state wouldn't let me because of my age and my heart. Her dad's family wanted her, too. They showed up at Sharon's funeral, and there was a big fight about it. But of course the state wasn't going to say yes. Not when Terry's family refused to even admit he'd killed Naomi. Child Protective Services was worried Terry would sneak back into town and his family would just hand Ariel over."

Everything stops.

So the argument at Grandma's funeral wasn't about how people didn't want me, but about how they did? It's happening again, the vase turning into the faces and then back into a vase. The center of my chest aches. With difficulty, I concentrate on what Nora is saying.

"We were all so sure we knew the truth, but we were wrong." She takes a deep breath. "Terry's funeral starts in forty-five minutes."

I nod, figuring out just now that Nora must be going. How am I going to go to the funeral without her wondering why I'm there?

She twists her hands again. "I don't know if I'll make it, though. I don't feel real sharp today. It's not that far, but I'm not sure I'm up to driving."

I realize Nora is both the problem and the solution.

"Why don't I give you a ride?"

CHAPTER 7

WHO ARE THESE PEOPLE?

AFTER OPENING THE CAR DOOR, NORA plops into the seat sideways. Turning, she slowly lifts each leg in, then finally closes the door and tells me which way to go. The cemetery is less than a mile away. The funeral home, a sprawling white building, sits on top of a small rise.

The parking lot is full. I hadn't expected more than a handful of people. I follow the drive around to a back lot and finally find a space. Someone has left a shopping cart full of junk at the end, but my car is small enough that I can tuck it in.

I should have let Nora out at the door. "Want me to go back and drop you off up front?"

She doesn't answer, just opens her door.

I hurry around to help. Nora's swung her legs out, but she's still sitting. I lean down, grab her forearms, and haul her upright. She grabs the crook of my arm, and we start to walk.

"Are you okay?" I ask. Nora's using me for more than just balance.

"I need to do this," she says, which isn't really an answer.

Despite her long legs, Nora's steps are short and slow. I match her pace. Around us, rows of flat metal grave markers are occasionally broken up by benches, marble statues, or little ponds. It's pretty here. Peaceful.

Maybe the woods where my dad has been all these years are peaceful, too. For a minute, I picture white snow lying like a fluffy blanket under evergreens so tall they crowd the sky.

I stop short.

Where did that come from? Was it even real?

Nora tugs my arm. "I'm not dead yet, honey." Catching sight of someone, she waves her arm. "Frank, you old geezer!"

An old man walks back to meet us. He's about my height, five foot seven, but as solid as a fire hydrant.

"Good to see you, Nora," he says, and then looks at me expectantly. I don't know what to say, but she does.

"This is Olivia. She's my guardian angel. This morning, I told God I didn't feel strong enough to come, and then Olivia turned up."

Outside the wooden doors, about a dozen people are chatting. Everyone's wearing dark colors, but no one looks like a movie mourner. My black T-shirt and pants aren't too out of place.

Frank is holding the door for us when a wiry old man with a cigarette calls his name. "Ladies," Frank says, before turning back.

The lobby is full of people milling around. Who are they? A lot of them look like they're about the ages my parents would be if they had lived.

The doors to the chapel stand open. In front are upholstered chairs, and behind them two men in suits are hurriedly setting up dozens of metal folding chairs.

In the center of the entryway stands an easel with a big photo of my dad wearing a cap and gown. His Adam's apple sticks out above the knot of a tie. Scattered around the room are more easels covered with snapshots. Some people are adding their own photos.

I walk straight to the nearest easel, my eyes darting from photo to photo. The only pictures I've seen of my dad are the ones on *America's Most Wanted*. I've never even thought about him as a kid. But here's my dad on a tricycle, a skateboard, a motocross bike. Holding a plastic bat. Always grinning, sometimes with missing baby teeth.

The pictures aren't in any order, so there's also one of my parents at the prom, standing stiffly next to a white pillar. And a photo of me holding my dad's hand at the beach. I wonder if it was taken the same day as the photo on *America's Most Wanted*. I have the blond springy curls I've only seen in photos. I'm fingering my dark waves when Nora's voice interrupts my thoughts. "Honey, would you mind terribly if I asked you to stay and give me a ride home?"

I turn back. "No problem at all."

She hesitates. "Only if you're sure. I could probably get Frank to take me."

"After hearing what happened, I'm curious." It's not really a lie, but still, I don't meet her eyes.

Nora takes my arm. "Do me a favor and help me get a seat before the mob rushes in."

In the chapel, the folding chairs are now all set up, and some people are already taking seats. Nora sits in the last row of upholstered chairs, then plops her purse onto the chair next to her. "I'll save this for you. Go look at the pictures. I saw some of my friend Sharon."

Back in the lobby, I bite on the insides of my cheeks to keep my face neutral, a trick I learned a long time ago.

My father at birthday parties, at restaurants, holding a blue can of Pabst.

Holding a silver fish, grinning.

Holding a limp deer by the antlers, grinning.

Maybe he liked to kill things. Maybe it hadn't been such a stretch to think he'd killed my mom. Or maybe this is just the kind of small town where people hunt and fish. I feel like I swallowed a stone. Who was my father, really?

A man's loud voice interrupts my thoughts. "Remember that time we were all in Terry's old car? Going a hundred and five miles an hour?" I turn. Even though most people are dressed casually, this guy has taken things one step further. Skinny, but with a barrel chest, he's dressed in flip-flops, shorts, and a multicolored Hawaiian shirt.

"It was a Trans Am, right?" The other man looks Asian, or maybe only half, with dark, straight hair and eyes that turn up at the corners. His charcoal suit, cut close to his slender body, boasts a gray silk pocket square. He doesn't look like he belongs in Medford, or even in Portland, but instead in Los Angeles—or maybe Tokyo.

"Don't you remember the Wasp, Rich?" Hawaiian Shirt Guy says. "Bright yellow with that black interior?"

Rich doesn't answer. His attention has shifted, as has everyone else's in the room. A girl wearing a black dress and sandals has just walked in, but it's not her clothes making people stare. It's her purple hair. That and the silver chain running from a ring in her right earlobe to a second ring in her nose.

"It's a funeral, for gosh sakes," an older woman behind me whispers. "She comes dressed like that to a funeral!"

I decide she looks perfectly fine if you take away the purple hair and the piercings. Even just the piercings. Maybe she doesn't want anyone to see past them.

I look back at the easel, then suck in my breath. In what must be a Thanksgiving photo, my dad sits at the head of a long table, with a turkey on a platter in front of him. He's joking around, looking maniacal, teeth gritted and shoulders hunched as he lifts his hand overhead, pretending to stab the turkey like a crazed slasher. Everyone else is laughing. Grandma and my mom and me on one side, Grandpa Jack and a young woman on the other. I'm sitting on my mom's lap. My mom is a little blurred because she was just starting to turn her head away.

The guy standing next to me looks at me curiously. He's about my age, with curly black hair and those thick eyelashes only guys seem to come by naturally.

"My parents had that exact same chair." I point at a green recliner at the edge of the photo. It's a lame excuse, but it's the best I can think of.

He follows my finger, looking a bit puzzled, and then we both go back to looking.

"I didn't think Sam would be here," a woman next to me whispers to another. I look where they are. They're not talking about a man, but a slender woman with shoulder-length blond hair and wide cheekbones. "Wasn't she dating Terry before he started seeing Naomi?"

"I heard it wasn't just before," the other woman says, her voice only slightly hushed. "She tried to get him to break up with Naomi."

She's scrawny, I decide. Scrawny, and her nose is too long. Realizing I'm staring, I turn back to look at more photos.

Me and my parents. I'm dressed for Halloween in a ballerina outfit defeated by cold weather. My pink net skirt comes down to my ankles. Under the narrow straps of my dress I'm wearing a hand-knit sweater that makes me look like a cross between a ballerina and a lumberjack. My mom is dressed in your standard cheap sexy nurse outfit. My dad's wearing red rubber hair and is made up like a clown. But I look happy. Happier than I ever remember being.

Six weeks later, two of the people in this photo were dead.

A man standing by the chapel doors clears his throat. "Okay, folks, if you could take your seats, the service will begin."

I'm at the easel farthest from the doors. As everyone shuffles inside, I unpin the photo and slip it into my back pocket.

CHAPTER 8

MY FATHER'S
LOST BONES

AN USHER HANDS ME A PROGRAM. ON THE
front is the photo of my dad in cap and gown. I hold it
carefully so it won't get wrinkled. I'm going to leave
Medford with two things—the photo in my pocket and
this.

That's all of my dad I'll ever have. That and a memory
of an apple he might have peeled for me. And the long
nose and square chin we share.

I scoot in next to Nora, exchange a smile with her, and
then look around. The cute guy is in the same row, but
on the other side of the room. For a second, his eyes catch
mine. I'm the first to look away.

In the back corner is a guy with straggly red hair and
a sunburned face. He's wearing a heavy coat that even
across the room looks filthy. He must own the shopping
cart my car is sharing a spot with.

Sam, my dad's maybe-ex-girlfriend, is sitting three
rows ahead of him. Her head is bowed, and one of her
hands is over her eyes.

The purple-haired girl is sitting in the front row, next to a woman whose photo I recognize from the *Medford Mail Tribune* website. It's my dad's sister, Carly. My aunt. So that girl must be my cousin. A man with silvered temples sits on the other side of Carly.

An organ begins to play, but it's a recording. A door hidden in the front wall opens, and a middle-aged guy in a suit with a white banded collar walks up to the podium. The music stops with a *click*.

"Good afternoon," the minister says. "We are gathered here today to remember Terry Weeks. While I never had the pleasure of knowing Terry, I have learned a lot about him this week. Terry was a friend. A neighbor. A coworker." He pauses between each pronouncement, his eyes surveying the chapel. "A brother." He nods at Carly, then at her daughter. "An uncle." His gaze sweeps over the rows. "A son. A boyfriend. A father."

I fight the urge to turn away as his gaze slides over me. The palms of my hands are sweaty. He doesn't know who I am, I remind myself. No one does.

"Let us pray."

I bow my head as he asks for comfort for the people here and eternal peace for my father's soul. As he prays, I wonder where my father's jawbone is. I imagine it in a white cardboard box marked EVIDENCE. Dirty and gray. Waiting to be reunited with the rest of his lost bones.

After the amen, the minister says, "The family has asked that we keep this memorial informal. They'd like to hear your memories of Terry, stories they can treasure as they heal. So please, come up to the microphone, introduce yourself, and tell us how you knew Terry and how you'll remember him."

After a pause, Sam walks up to the microphone, moving so stiffly it's as if her knees don't work. Head down, blond hair falling over her eyes, she turns to face the crowd. Her voice is hoarse and soft. "If you wanted to have fun, all you had to do was hang out with Terry. He loved football games, concerts, parties, and, of course, going down to the river. I can still see him standing on the shore in his orange swim trunks, yelling out, 'Where've you guys been? I've been waiting for you for so long!' That's how I've felt about him for the last fourteen years." Her shoulders round over, shaking.

I watch and wonder. That detective said my mom might have been stabbed so many times because the killer knew her. He even said it could have been a woman. What if Sam killed my mother in a jealous rage and then turned on my dad when he tried to stop her?

My eyes sweep the room. Is everyone really here to mourn my father? Or does someone know—or guess—who killed him? Could the killer even be here? The press of bodies and the warm air make me feel claustrophobic.

The businessman walks up and gives Sam's shoulder a quick squeeze, then takes the microphone from her. "I'm Richard Lee. Terry and I used to pal around back in the day. He loved animals and the outdoors, but most of all, he loved his family. He loved his dad and you, Carly, and of course Naomi, and their daughter, Ariel. I pray you will finally find peace."

The guy in the Hawaiian shirt is up next. "Hey. I'm

Jason. You guys all probably know I was Terry's best friend. I'll always remember that big grin of his. And he was forever telling those stupid jokes that took way too long to tell and ended with punch lines like 'Arty Chokes Three for a Dollar.'" People laugh.

Jason's expression turns serious. "I was going to be the best man at Terry and Naomi's wedding. They hadn't set a date, but I'm sure they would have done it. Maybe even had more kids. Sure, they had their daughter way too young. But Terry stepped up. And he was so proud to be a dad." He falls quiet for a moment, and the microphone picks up how his breathing hitches. "No one knows what happened in the woods that day. But I'll tell you one thing: I know in my heart that Terry died trying to protect his family." He looks up at the ceiling. "I hope we'll meet at a party up in heaven, dude."

So proud to be a dad. The thought warms me.

Nora and I exchange a smile, although she probably thinks I'm smiling at Jason's use of the word *dude*.

For years, I've felt so alone. Abandoned by everyone. By my mother, who was stupid enough to have a child with a man who would soon kill her. By my father, who was worse than dead. By a woman who said she wanted to be my mom but who couldn't see how much I was hurting.

But those first two things weren't true. And now I'm sitting next to an old woman who loved my grandmother. Who loved my mother. Who once loved me.

Here, things feel like they fit into gaps I didn't even know I had. An empty space shaped like the golden hills that hold this valley. A hollow filled by the woman next to me, a woman with silver hair and crowded teeth. Maybe there are even three missing pieces shaped like my aunt and uncle and their purple-haired daughter.

The next man at the microphone wears a uniform and badge. Even without them, I would know he's a cop or a soldier, with his squared shoulders and too-short brown hair. "I'm Stephen Spaulding, the chief of police. I'd known Naomi since kindergarten, and I met Terry when they started dating. After they went missing, and again when Naomi's body was found, I was part of the group called out to search for them." He looks up, his face reddening. "Terry, brother, I'm sorry we didn't find you." He blows air through pursed lips, and his face is sad. "I promise you're not forgotten. Neither one of you."

A tall woman with auburn hair and pale skin has been waiting for her turn at the microphone. "I'm Heather. I was Naomi's best friend. She and Terry started dating in high school. They were in love from the moment their eyes met. But being in love never stopped them from fighting. And when Naomi was found, I thought the worst. I spent years hating Terry for taking her from us." Heather glances up at the ceiling. She's another person with something to say and no one to say it to. "I'm sorry, Terry. I was wrong to ever think that. I hope you can forgive me."

With lips pressed together, Carly takes the microphone from her. "I'm Carly, Terry's older sister. Our mom died from breast cancer when we were little, but Terry was always Daddy's boy. Terry and my dad were more like best friends than father and son. My dad never stopped searching, but part of him died the day they found Naomi's body. Not because he thought Terry did it but because he knew Terry had to be dead, too. My dad always believed my brother was innocent. He never wavered. Not once." She takes a shaky breath. "I have to confess I did. Once or twice. But then I'd realize that he'd never abandon his little girl like that. It just breaks my heart to think about Ariel. I sent her a letter care of her old caseworker but haven't heard back yet. I'm sure she's still coming to terms with things, the way the rest of us are." Her unsteady breathing fills the room. "When the police told me they found Terry's jawbone, I felt like my soul had been ripped from my body. I didn't know it could still hurt this much."

So much pain. Samantha's and Jason's and Richard's. Tim's and Heather's and Carly's. Friends, relatives, and neighbors. Whoever killed my parents hurt so many people.

Including me.

When everyone is done speaking, the pastor says, "Let us pray," and people bow their heads. "God of merciful love, help Terry's friends and family remember the joyful times they shared while he was still on this earth. Teach them the forgiveness that was exemplified by Jesus as he said, 'Father, forgive them, for they know not what they do.'"

He's not done praying, but I'm done listening. I open my eyes.

I'm not going to forgive. Someone murdered my parents and left them underneath the cold sky and thought they got away with it.

They were wrong.

CHAPTER 9

WATCHING EVERYONE

I TAKE A SIP OF LEMONADE. IT TASTES LIKE chemicals. I've stationed myself in the corner across from the tables of snacks that have been set up in the lobby. The homeless guy scurries away. Clutched to his chest is a paper plate piled high with crackers, cheese slices, baby carrots, and Oreo cookies.

"Benjy!" Nora calls out, waving at him as people's heads turn, but he keeps going until he's through the doors. He's not as old as I first thought. Did he know my dad, or does he just crash funerals, hoping to score free food?

The tears people cried earlier seem to have freed them to smile and even laugh. I hear talk about the upcoming football season, how hot it is, and who's having a baby.

On paper, these people are my dad's friends, relatives, old girlfriends, coworkers, and neighbors. But is one of them also his killer?

Carrying a plate heaped with food, Sam comes away from the table. Maybe she wanted my dad back, and my mom was standing in the way. Only my dad hadn't appreciated Sam's problem solving, and she'd had to kill him, too. But she's so skinny. Would she even have been strong enough to stab my mom so many times?

I look around the room. Who else might know what really happened? Nora is deep in conversation with Jason, my dad's old best friend. She's got one arm around his back like she's comforting him.

In the opposite corner, Frank is talking to Richard Lee—or rather *at* him, shaking his finger.

I'm so busy watching everyone that I don't see the cute guy I noticed earlier until he's a few feet away. He holds out a paper plate with a stem of green grapes, two slices of cheese, four strawberries, and a half dozen Ritz crackers.

"Here. This is for you."

"What?" I take a half step back until my shoulders brush the wall. "Why?"

"I thought you might be hungry." Some guys would say that like there's a double meaning, but I think he means just what he says. Plus I *am* hungry. It's after three, and I haven't eaten since I grabbed some Lucky Charms this morning. Just looking at the cheese makes my mouth fill with water.

"My name's Duncan."

I have to juggle the plate and cup so I can stick out my hand. "Olivia."

Duncan looks a bit flustered but finally shakes my hand. "So how did you know Terry?"

"Actually, I didn't." It hurts me that this isn't even a lie. "I just gave the old lady over there a ride." I point at Nora.

One side of his mouth turns up in a lopsided grin. "Nora? An old lady? It's kind of weird to think of her like that."

"Sorry." I know what he means, though. Even though she *is* old, she doesn't seem like other old people. I try to turn it into a joke. "I mean, that honored citizen in her golden years." Nora now has her arm looped through Jason's, and they're singing what sounds like a Christmas carol, more or less in harmony. Duncan and I exchange a smile, and some of my sorrow lifts.

"Did you know Terry?" It's kind of a silly question, since Duncan looks about my age. Then again, he *is* at my dad's funeral.

"I grew up next to Terry's dad, Mr. Weeks, but my parents knew Terry. They bought our house before I was born, while Terry was still in high school." He bites into a cracker and adds, "He and his girlfriend had a little girl, you know."

I keep my eyes steady on his. Duncan's eyes are beautiful, gray with a black ring around the edge. "I heard about her."

"My parents said Terry used to bring her over to play when we were little."

Mud houses, I think. Mud mixed with grass clippings and left to dry in the rough shape of walls. Only I just don't think it—I know it. I can feel the texture between my hands. The memory is so unexpected it steals my breath. I manage a nod.

"How do you know Nora?" he asks.

"I'm thinking of renting the house next door. Nora saw me looking at it and came over. Since she wasn't feeling well, I offered her a ride."

Could I really rent it? The rental-management company still transfers the money to Ariel Benson, and through some magic at the bank, the payments show up in my account. As far as I know, the rental people don't even know there is an Olivia Reinhart.

"So you might move into the house Terry's girlfriend lived in?"

I nod. "That's the other reason I came today. I got curious after Nora told me about what happened. Which is sort of wrong, I guess."

My face is calm, but my thoughts are racing. If I rent the house my grandma left me, the money will eventually come back to me, less the management company's fee. By giving up my apartment in Portland, I'd actually end up several hundred dollars a month ahead. I'd just need to work enough for gas and food. And Top Ramen doesn't cost that much.

Duncan waves his hand at the room. "I don't think a lot of these people knew Terry that well. It's more that they're curious. This is a pretty big deal in Medford."

"People don't get killed here?"

He shrugs. "Oh, they get killed all the time, but it's the usual: drunk people arguing, men killing their girlfriends or wives, maybe something gang-related. But not two people mysteriously murdered in the woods years ago. Plus, my parents say the whole town feels guilty. For years, everyone believed Terry killed Naomi. And for years, everyone was wrong."

CHAPTER 10

I REMEMBER

"I'M GOING TO GRAB A COUPLE MORE cookies," Duncan says. As I follow him over to the table, I find myself looking at everyone and wondering.

He has just picked up an Oreo when a woman's voice raps out, "Hey—you put that back!"

He drops the cookie as if it's on fire.

But it's just Nora. She's standing across from us, grinning. "I already called dibs on it," she says.

I'm not used to old people joking around. Most of the senior citizens who shop at my Fred Meyer store are as bland as pastel sweaters.

"Finders keepers, Nora." Duncan retrieves the cookie. It's gone in two bites. He turns back to me. "Where are you from?"

Another answer pops out of my mouth. "Seattle." Not thinking things through is working for me. I've been to Seattle on the train a couple of times, so I can fake it.

"Cool. What neighborhood?"

What neighborhood, what neighborhood? "Pretty close to

the Space Needle." Except a view of the Space Needle is probably expensive, so I add, "Not that you can see it from my apartment."

Luckily, my answer seems to satisfy him. "So why'd you come down here?"

"The cost of living is a lot cheaper." That part's not a lie. "I'm taking a year off to save for college." My patchwork of answers is getting thin, but Duncan doesn't seem to notice.

Nora saves me by saying, "Ready to take me home, Olivia?"

"Sure. Just let me go to the bathroom first." I turn to Duncan. "It was nice talking to you."

"Maybe I'll stop by next time I'm over at Nora's."

"Okay." I feel a little thrill. He grins at me and then goes over to talk to Frank.

Nora puts her arm around my shoulder and squeezes. "Oh, so you've decided to stay? I'm so glad. It will be wonderful being neighbors."

"Yeah," I say, stepping back. I'm not used to being touched. "I'll be right back."

As I'm going into the bathroom, Sam is coming out. Her face is flushed and blotchy, as if she's been crying. The bathroom is otherwise empty. Right after I slide the bolt in the far corner stall, two women come in.

"Everyone was asking me about the holes in your face." I recognize Carly's voice. And it's not hard to guess who she's talking to as they go into the stalls.

"It's my face," the girl retorts. "Not yours, not theirs. Mine."

Carly's voice is tight. "You could have honored your uncle by at least taking off that ridiculous chain."

"From what I remember of Uncle Terry, he would have thought I was badass."

"Lauren!"

"It's not like I showed up pregnant or something. And besides, that's why people are here. So they can gossip. So what does it matter what I wear or what color my hair is? It doesn't hurt Uncle Terry, and it gave them something to talk about."

"It matters because it affects people's opinions of you," my aunt says.

"If they can't look past a six-inch-long sterling-silver chain, then I don't care what they think."

They both flush at the same time, and then I hear the sounds of hands being washed and the main door opening and closing. After that it's quiet, so I flush and come out.

But Lauren's still there. Her eyes look wet. She bites her lip and turns away.

There's no use pretending I didn't hear them arguing. "I like your hair," I say. It's the truth, too. "I like that shade of purple."

Her expression softens. "Thanks. You know moms. They're never happy." Her voice turns singsong. "*What did you do to your hair? When's the last time you ate something healthy? Who's that boy I saw you talking to?*" She rolls her eyes.

"Yeah," I echo. "Moms." I nod and then leave.

When I come out, Nora's sitting in a chair, her head

49

hanging low. She brightens when she sees me. I loop her big black purse over my shoulder and help her to her feet.

"I'm so glad you're going to be next door," she declares. "You'll love that house."

"I'll call the rental company today."

We both fall silent as we walk out the big doors.

"So," she finally says. "Duncan."

"What about Duncan?" Just saying his name makes my heart beat a little faster.

"That's what I wanted to ask you." Nora raises one eyebrow.

"I just met him." I try to tamp down my smile. "He seems nice."

"Nice," she echoes. "That's like when the best thing you can say about a girl is that she sews all her own clothes."

"But I don't know him."

"Mmm-hmm," Nora says, but it sounds as though she's really disagreeing with me.

Back at her house, I park and help her out. As she goes up her walk, I stand in front of the rental sign and dial the number for Lee Realty.

The phone rings three times before a woman answers. I take a breath, but then I realize it's just a recording. After the beep, I say, "My name is Olivia Reinhart, and I'd like to talk to you about renting the property at 1707 Terrace Drive." I end with my cell phone number.

If the rental company isn't open on a Saturday afternoon, it's surely not going to be open tomorrow. Now what? Maybe I can find a quiet road and lock the car doors and sleep there the next two nights. I don't want to waste money on a motel.

Nora speaks, and I realize she hasn't gone inside. "Can't get hold of them?"

"The office is closed."

"Then you should stay with me until Monday."

I shake my head. "That's okay. I'll find a motel or something."

"Nonsense. I have a guest room, and you'll be my guest." She turns as if it's already decided. Without looking to see if I'm following, she goes inside. After a moment, I follow her.

Until today, I didn't even remember Nora. And if you had asked me what the inside of Nora's house looked like, I would have said I had no idea. It turns out I do and I don't.

It's like I'm in one of those snow globes. Somebody's picked me up and shaken all my memories loose. Now they float around me, flickering in the corners of my eyes.

Just inside the door sits a blue flowered couch topped with a nest of afghans. An old wingback chair, upholstered in gold brocade, stands at a right angle to it. I don't need to look to know its feet are carved wooden talons gripping balls.

Nora's house is crammed with books, colored bottles, baskets, and hanging plants. The walls are covered with things in frames: photos, little paintings, shells, and a tiny ivory elephant, as well as an old silver-backed brush, a carved walnut on a miniature hook, and a brass clock that ticks in the hot stillness. Everything's a little dusty, a little chipped. Stuffed with so many knickknacks, Nora's house should be suffocating, but instead it's like a mosaic, all the pieces coming together in a pleasing whole.

While I'm taking it all in, Nora sits down in a dining room chair and toes off her shoes, then gets up and puts them in a closet. Moving slowly, she walks to the couch. When she sits, it's more like a well-cushioned fall. She pulls fake UGG sheepskin-lined boots over her socks and then arranges the afghans over her lap.

It's got to be at least ninety degrees in here. But I remember what she said about her heart, how cold her hands were.

I take the brocade chair. "I was wondering, if Terry's buried at that cemetery, is Naomi there, too?" I want to visit my mother's grave.

"Naomi and Sharon are in Odd Fellows. The other cemetery."

"Medford has more than one?" The city seems so small.

"Odd Fellows was here first. It's just around the corner. Sharon always liked it better. People have picnics there, and it's where every teenager learns to drive." Nora's eyes crinkle when she smiles. "You can't kill anyone in a cemetery. They're already dead."

The word *dead* leads me right back to my parents. "Who do you think really did it?" I ask her. "Everyone there seemed to know you. You must have some ideas."

"People in this town hold their secrets pretty close."

"You don't think it was a stranger, then?"

Nora looks at me for a long moment. "No." But she doesn't say anything more.

We watch the news together. For dinner, she has me

heat up canned tomato soup and warm frozen rolls in the oven. She says she used to like to bake but doesn't have the energy anymore. *I remember,* I want to say, but I keep the words stoppered tight.

．We watch a documentary about birds of paradise. They're like no birds I've ever seen, with crazy-colored feathers, beaks, and even feet. When the show ends at nine, Nora goes to bed, and so do I. I'm sure I'll be awake for hours, but my eyelids are so heavy they close by themselves.

CHAPTER 11

WICKED POINT

IT'S COLD. NEXT TO ME, SOMEONE IS muttering under their breath, but I don't look. I won't. I'm curled on my side away from them, my eyes closed, my thumb in my mouth. I'm too old to suck my thumb. But it feels good. I like how it fits into the roof of my mouth like it belongs there, like the space was made special just to fit it.

I pull it out with a pop. When I open my eyes, my thumb is all wrinkled and wet. And past it, I see a knife lying on the carpet. It has a wooden handle and a blade that curves down to a wicked point. But it's not the knife that makes me scream.

It's the blood drying on the blade.

"Olivia!"

I have to get away. I scramble back until my shoulders hit a wall.

"Olivia!" Nora says again. Her silver hair brushes my face. "Olivia! You're having a nightmare."

My whole body is slick with sweat. My breath comes in gasps.

The knife. The knife, the blood, the muttering.
The knife.

I was dreaming about being in the killer's car.

Or was it a memory, not a dream?

"Sorry," I groan. I pull the sheet over my bare legs. I must have kicked it off.

"What were you dreaming about?"

Something about her gaze makes me tell the truth. At least part of it. "About that guy Terry and his girlfriend. It would be so awful to be murdered. To know that you're dying and that the last thing you see will be your killer."

Nora sits on the edge of the bed. She's so thin the mattress doesn't even dip.

She pats my knee through the sheet. "Oh, honey, I'm sorry if I made a mistake asking you to take me to the funeral. And as much as I would love to have you as a neighbor, maybe you shouldn't rent that house. After all, Naomi lived there. I don't want you waking up screaming every night."

"It's not like she would be haunting it." Although, could some part of her spirit still linger? I would love to be able to talk to my mother, even her ghost. To have her answer, even in my dreams. "Besides, you said that house has lots of good memories."

"Oh, it does. It does." Her forehead is still furrowed. "Still, I'm sorry I exposed you to the evil in this world, Olivia. You should stay ignorant of that as long as you can."

"I'm not a little kid. I already know about evil." Nineteen stab wounds, a jawbone, blood drying on a knife. I know a lot about evil.

Nora gives me a long look. "Yes, I suppose you do." She bows her head, and I realize that she's saying a prayer. "Lord, help Olivia to have a restful sleep tonight."

She's on her feet before I can decide whether to say "amen."

But I can't go back to sleep. Not when my mind might finally be beginning to shake loose what really happened. Maybe there are other clues from my dream besides the knife. Like the carpet it was lying on. What color was it? That might be important. Tan? Blue? But each possibility seems as real as any other.

What about the person I heard muttering? Was it a man or a woman?

I don't know. All I remember is they sounded crazy.

This is the second snippet of memory I've had since I got here. First the snowy woods and now this. I guess if they're real, they're flashbacks. But they haven't shown me anything I could go to the police about. For that, I need facts.

And maybe I'm just making the whole thing up. Filling in the blanks. My subconscious telling me what I've already been thinking: that to kill two people, you have to be some sort of crazy. That stabbing someone so many times does not go hand in hand with sanity.

I don't know whether to trust this memory or my overactive imagination or whatever it is. I'm still thinking this when I fall into a deep and, thankfully, dreamless sleep.

Is there anything better than the smell of bacon? I wake with a damp spot on the pillow. I've been drooling in my sleep.

I straighten the bed, put on clean clothes, and then find Nora in the kitchen. She turns when I walk in. "Good morning, *sweat* heart." She grins at her own joke. Her hair is pinned back, and she's wearing a navy polyester tunic and pants. Around her throat is a necklace made of what at first I think are beads. When I take a closer look, I see they are buttons in all different shades of blue, from sea to midnight.

"Oh, that's beautiful!"

She touches the necklace with one of her age-spotted hands. "You like it?"

"It's gorgeous."

Before I realize what she's doing, she's pulled it over her head and is holding it out to me. "Then it's yours."

I take a step back. "That's okay."

Nora keeps holding out the necklace. "It didn't really cost me anything. I buy old buttons at garage sales and string them while I'm watching the news." She presses the necklace into my hand.

"I can't take it," I say, but I don't let go. The buttons are cool and smooth, knotted onto what looks like dental floss. "You've already done too much for me."

"Nonsense. If you weren't here, I would be talking to myself. It's not easy living alone."

"Do you have kids or anything?" I slip on the necklace.

"A boy and a girl. But they both grew up and moved away a long time ago. My daughter lives in Bozeman, Montana, with her husband and my twelve-year-old granddaughter. My son lives in Seattle with his boyfriend. They both call a lot, but it's not like having someone in the house. And my husband died almost ten years ago.

Which is why I talk to myself." A rueful smile flits across her face. "It's when you start answering back that you know you're in trouble." She changes the subject. "Would you like to go to church with me this morning? And it's okay to say no."

I haven't been to church in years, not since I was living with foster parents who made us all go twice on Sundays and on Wednesday nights as well. "Maybe not today?" My voice rises at the end, making it a question.

Nora smiles. "Then I guess it's time for bacon and coffee."

My cheeks feel hot. "That sounds good."

She pulls a red jar from the fridge, then dumps some brown crystals into a coffee cup. From the old brass kettle on the stove, she adds hot water. Instant coffee. I resolve to drink it down fast. Meanwhile, Nora takes a plate from the microwave and peels back a layer of paper towels to reveal strips of bacon. She puts six crisp strips on a plate and hands it to me, then takes a carton of eggs from the fridge. "Scrambled okay?"

"That would be great. Can I help?"

"Could you read me the headlines instead?" She points at a rolled-up newspaper sitting on the counter. "And then I'll tell you which stories to read all the way through."

It turns out Nora's interested in everything except sports. I read her stories in between bites of bacon. The six strips, which seemed like far too much, are gone in a few bites.

A fifty-five-year-old woman was found dead at her house, and the police want to talk to her ex-husband. Fire danger is extremely high, and hikers are being warned not to light campfires. A burglar hit a half dozen busi-nesses on East Main Street. A couple has started a business making casseroles to go.

Between the woman's murder and the burglaries, it sounds like the police chief has his hands full. With no new clues, how hard will he work to figure out who killed my parents?

Nora mounds eggs on my plate. It's a weird feeling, being waited on. In most of the foster homes I was in, we either poured our own cereal or ate the free breakfast at school. If my family had lived, would I be used to this? After I finish eating, Nora allows me to wash the dishes.

"If I go on a walk while you're at church, how should I lock the door?" I ask as I put the last dish in the drainer.

Nora shrugs. "Don't worry about it. There's nothing here worth stealing. I never lock up during the day."

Medford's small, but it's not that small. She's living in some olden time that doesn't exist, and hasn't for decades. But then again, she's right. Her huge old TV, her heaps of afghans, her dining room chairs that aren't quite steady on their legs—who would want them?

To me, Nora's house is full of things I long for. But none of them are tangible.

CHAPTER 12

STANDING ON YOUR BONES

I PUSH OPEN THE CEMETERY'S METAL GATE. The three vertical bars are decorated with two oversize oak leaves made of copper. A sign says it's a designated historic site.

This cemetery is more hilly than the other one. The roads are unpaved, just two tracks of gravel. Instead of well-manicured grass, there are only weeds and wild-flowers.

Ahead, the road splits in two. The section on the right holds only a few graves and slopes gently to a wooden fence.

Us kids used to ride our sleds down that hill. This is a real memory from when I was six or seven, not a dream or my imagination. My grandma leaning over to give me a push. Me laughing and gasping, joy and fear mixed together, my fingers curled tight around the wooden edge of the sled, the snow only inches from my face. Running back to her, shouting, "Again! Again!"

Now the same ground is being mowed by an old man

wearing sunglasses and a battered straw cowboy hat. He raises a leather-gloved hand from the tractor's steering wheel. I return the gesture.

No wonder my grandmother chose this place for my mom instead of the sterile flat grass where my father is buried. This jumble of weathered stones of all shapes and sizes makes the other one look as appealing as a filing cabinet.

I don't remember where my mom's grave is, so I let my feet choose which way to walk, which turns out to be up the hill toward a big stucco building with stained-glass windows. Along the way, I pause to read grave-stones. Now that I'm here, I'm in no hurry to be confronted with the chiseled words that will permanently underline the truth.

One small white marble marker says just the word *Baby* and the dates of its birth and death, which are the same: May 7, 1904. At one point, a lamb must have deco-rated the top, but the head's been broken off.

The air is filled with the trills and chirps of birds, punctuated with the occasional caw of a blue jay. And then I hear the sad, distinctive call of a mourning dove rise and fall: *ooooh, ooh, ooh, ooh.* When I was a kid, I thought it was *morning*, not *mourning*, but then Grandma set me straight, explaining what the word meant.

Mourning. It's such an old-fashioned word, but so is *grief.* Both as heavy and solid as tombstones.

Each of these stones marks a person who was loved and missed. How many tears has this ground soaked up? Four children from the same family all died in July 1899. In 1936, a young woman died the same day as her newborn son. Here's Silas Hawk, who was twenty-one—the same age as my dad—when he died in 1919. Did he have a sweetheart? A child?

A few plots are surrounded by black wrought-iron fences complete with little gates. Small, plain gravestones stand next to those with elaborately carved birds and flowers, crowns and candles, doves and angels. One concrete monument is shaped like a tree shading a bench, and I maneuver closer to see the inscription. The weeds are as high as my ankle, and my foot slips into a small, crumbling hole. With a muffled cry, I yank it out. I know it's some animal's burrow, that no bony hand is going to come reaching out. That I can't thrust my arm down to touch moldering flesh. I know that.

This part of the cemetery hasn't yet been visited by the man with the tractor. Scattered among the graves are blue bachelor's buttons, orange poppies, white clumps of yarrow, yellow buttercups. In my head, I hear Grandma's voice as she names the wildflowers. Others are just plain weeds, full of thorns and stickers, not worthy of being remembered by name.

My eye is drawn by a flash of orange. It's not a spectacular wildflower but an unopened bag of Cheetos. I know even before I get close enough to see that the marker belongs to my mom. Memories flood me, of how I would visit with already-drooping flowers picked from Grandma's yard. Sometimes my mother's friends had been there before us, and we would find a full bottle of beer or another offering. Once it was a rhinestone tiara, which Grandma allowed me to wear home.

Who brought the Cheetos? Who still remembers she

liked them? I've read that Chinese people sometimes burn play paper money, food, and clothing at the graves of their loved ones, believing the essence of the needed thing wafts to the afterlife.

I stand in front of the tombstones for my mother and my grandmother. They are nearly identical, even though they died four years apart.

Mommy, I am standing on your bones. Under my feet, she lies in a slowly rotting casket, with all the weight of the earth on her.

A cry is torn from my throat. *Mommy, mommy, mommy,* and then I'm on the dry, stony ground, pricker bushes scratching my face, but I don't care, tears hot on my cheeks. My words are jumbled, some in my head and some torn from my mouth. *Why did you have to leave me, why did they take you from me, why did they take everything, I miss you, I wish you were here, I love you, I'm so sorry I couldn't save you.*

I cry for a long time, at first so hard I can't catch my breath, and then slower and softer. Until finally I'm cried out, silent, stretched flat on her grave. My arms spread as if they might tunnel through the earth and pull her to me, reclaim her bones and put flesh on them.

And then I'm rewarded. No, I don't hear her voice in my ear. I don't feel her soft touch on my back. What I'm given is a memory. Of sitting on her lap and turning the pages of a book. "'Brown bear, brown bear what do you see?'" Her cheek against mine and her soft breath in my ear and her smell, a certain sweet smell, in my nose.

And for a moment I know without question I was loved.

But that doesn't make it any better. Because I was loved and someone took that from me. I cry again, more softly, the anger and rage bleeding away, leaving behind only a grief like a stone. I sleep then, without meaning to.

And wake to a rough hand on my shoulder.

CHAPTER 13

WHO'S GOING TO FIGURE OUT THE TRUTH?

"HONEY," A MAN'S VOICE SAYS HESITANTLY. "Are you okay?"

It's the second time today I've been awakened by an old person. This time, it's the guy in the battered straw cowboy hat. His riding mower, now silent, stands in the road behind him.

"I'm fine." I sit up, blinking in the bright sunshine. The dream I was having slips away. A man's voice, urging me forward. A hand on the back of my head.

"I could have mowed you down." He offers me a hand. "Here, get up. It can't be comfortable down there." Although he must be close to eighty, he has the strong grip of a workingman. His jeans sit high on his waist and end a couple of inches above his Velcro-closed tennis shoes.

I know him. It's Frank. Nora's friend. He was at my dad's—

"You were at the funeral," I say after he pulls me to

my feet. Will he put two and two together? Can he tell I've been crying? Maybe he'll just think I'm a weird teenager.

"That's right. I knew Terry. I also knew his girlfriend, Naomi." He looks down at the graves. "Naomi and her mom, Sharon."

"I'm thinking of renting their old house." I lean down to brush prickers off my pants, giving me an excuse not to look him in the face. "Nora told me they were buried here, so I thought I'd come visit the graves. But it's just so hot. I started feeling sleepy. I must have dozed off."

His face expressionless, Frank says, "Around this place, when we say someone's taking a dirt nap, it means they're dead and buried."

I stare at him for a second before I realize he's making a joke.

"Well, I'm not dead. Not yet."

He looks at the two graves again, and his mouth turns down at the corners. "Naomi—she wasn't much older than you." He shakes his head. "Sometimes it's hard to understand why someone so young dies but an old codger like me keeps going."

"What was she like?" I ask. "Naomi, I mean?"

"Young. She and Terry were too young to have a baby, but they did. Sharon wasn't happy about that."

I look down at my flat stomach, try to imagine a baby curled up under my skin. How did my mom feel? Scared? Happy? Both?

"She was a high-spirited gal," Frank continues. "Beautiful, like her mother."

I realize he means Grandma. I do the math. Grandma was only fifty-six when she died. If she were alive, she'd still be younger than him. "Were you working here when Naomi was murdered?" All those people who left things on her grave—could her killer have been one of them?

"I'd just started volunteering. For the first year after she died, people came here all the time. Sometimes they'd leave bottles of beer. Candy, snacks, Christmas ornaments."

"I found those Cheetos." I point at the bag.

He nods. "Every now and then I'll find just one red rose. I used to think it might be Terry sneaking back into town, but obviously not."

I'd always thought my mom belonged to my dad and vice versa, even if they weren't married. But now there's this Sam person who loved my dad, and some mystery man who still thinks about my mom. Could the rose be from her killer?

"So people still come?"

"I've seen a few. Naomi's best friend, this redheaded gal named Heather, she still comes around. There's a homeless guy who likes to sleep here. Sometimes I've seen him talking to Naomi's gravestone. And the police chief—he comes by sometimes, too. He was here last week, right after they figured out it was Terry's jawbone." Frank sighs. "Before she died, Sharon used to come here with her granddaughter. Naomi's kid, Ariel. Sometimes they had picnics right on top of the grave."

I will my expression not to change. "What do you think happened to Naomi and Terry?"

His lips fold in on themselves. His face is a mass of wrinkles, like a piece of paper that's been balled up and smoothed out a hundred times. "Maybe they took some-one with them that day."

I hadn't thought of that. That would mean it had to be a friend. Who's going to figure out the truth of what happened all these years later? I think of the police chief, his voice choked with tears. Apologizing for not finding my dad fourteen years ago. But it's clear from the articles in the paper that he has his hands full.

Frank leans down and picks up the Cheetos.

"What are you going to do with them?"

"Throw them away. They'll just attract varmints."

"Wait a second." I grab the bag and check the date. The Cheetos won't expire for three more weeks.

Frank cocks his head. "What are you looking at?"

"I'm just trying to figure out how long this has been here. Before or after people knew the truth about that Terry guy."

"Oh, it was after. I pick up stuff like this as soon as I notice it. Leaving food out here is just a bad idea. But people do it all the time."

Only now do I wonder if there were fingerprints on the bag, fingerprints we must have just destroyed. Although who's to say who put the bag here? It could just be one of my mom's friends. It probably wasn't the killer.

"I guess I'd better be getting back." I act as if there's somewhere I have to be. "It was nice talking to you."

He nods. "Same here."

Before I go, Frank reaches into his pocket and scatters a handful of yellow birdseed on my mother's and grand-mother's gravestones. A blue jay lights on a branch above us, and then another and another. They bob lightly in the breeze, too scared—or maybe too smart—to take the chance of eating while we're so close. They watch and wait for us to go away.

Just waiting until our backs are turned, our attention diverted.

CHAPTER 14

DOUBT A GIRL

WHEN I STEP INSIDE FRED MEYER ON Monday, the store is both familiar and not. It's like when I look at Nora and see the old Nora just underneath. This Fred Meyer has the same typeface on the signs as the store where I work, the same store-brand groceries sitting next to the name brand, but the pharmacy is in a different corner, the electronics section is bigger, and there are two more aisles of toys. It's like when you dream about a familiar place, but the dream version isn't the same.

"Where can I find the PIC?" I ask the guy behind the electronics counter. He has a few strands of gray hair swirled around his mostly bare scalp.

His brows draw together at the sound of store lingo coming out of the mouth of someone he doesn't know. *PIC* means "person in charge." He points. "His office is down that hall, past the restrooms."

The hall smells like bleach. Shallow plastic bins mounted on the walls hold job applications, workers' comp forms, and vacation request forms. A sign between the restrooms warns against taking merchandise inside. At the end of the hall is an unmarked door, and after a moment's hesitation, I knock on it.

"Come in," a voice barks. I open the door. The man behind the desk is stocky, with a shaved head and pale blue eyes.

With what I hope is a professional and friendly smile, I put out my hand. If I'm going to stay in Medford, I need to find a job before I do anything else. "I'm Olivia Reinhart. I wanted to ask if you have any openings."

"Chuck Tobart." He barely squeezes my hand before releasing it, his eyes already going back to the paperwork on his desk. "Forms are out in the hall."

"I'm hoping to transfer. I work at the Burlingame Freddy's."

He looks at me again. "Up in Portland?"

"Yeah. In the deli." I slice cheese and meats and encourage people to try samples. It isn't a bad job. Our manager, Bill, always lets me have day-old stuff for free. And when he found out that I got off work five minutes after the bus left and that it didn't come again for another hour, he shifted my schedule back without my asking.

"How long have you worked there?"

"Seven months."

"I don't have an opening in the deli." He says it like the conversation is already at an end.

"I'll do anything. Even be a cart jockey." Pushing carts is the worst job. Your shins and hips are bruised from bucking carts together or apart, from shoving them in huge clumps across the parking lot. "I'm moving down here, and I need a job. I'll work as many hours as you give me, and I'll work hard."

He cocks his head. "Aren't you still in school?"

I let Duncan think I was a year older, but there's no point in lying to the manager about my age, because the other store will give it to him. "I've got my GED."

"The only opening I have is in produce." His lips twist. "And I doubt a girl your size could lift fifty pounds."

Not only is fifty pounds a lot, but produce boxes are usually big, making it hard to use your legs instead of your arms and back.

"I'm really strong." I'm stretching the truth and worried it sounds more like a flat-out lie.

He grunts, unconvinced. "Fill out the form, and I'll talk to your manager up in Portland."

My manager. Crap. The first thing I need to do is call Bill and give him a heads-up. I know Bill likes me—but will that change when he learns I'm planning on leaving him in the lurch?

It's possible I could end up with no job at all.

CHAPTER 15

DON'T TELL ME

IN FRONT OF LEE REALTY, A BILLBOARD-SIZE sign says LET RICHARD LEE LEAD YOU HOME. A smiling headshot of the Asian guy at my dad's funeral is superimposed on a collage of beautiful homes. Even though Richard Lee grew up with my parents, I can't imagine they were headed for anything like his success. I get out of my car, trying not to think about how my gas gauge is hovering near *E*.

The office is spacious, all clean lines and windows. Just walking across the long expanse of mustard-gold carpet to the front desk makes me nervous. A half wall of marble, topped with a potted yellow orchid, separates me from the receptionist. She's talking on her headset.

When she says, "Yes?" it takes me a minute to realize she's addressing me. Her eyes are still on her computer screen.

"Um, hi. I want to talk to someone about renting 1707 Terrace?" My stomach clenches.

"Your name?"

"Olivia Reinhart."

She finds an application and hands it over with a pen, all without her eyes ever leaving her screen. "Fill this out. I'll tell Christina you're here."

I sit on the edge of one of four pristine white upholstered chairs clustered around a gleaming coffee table and use a copy of *Architectural Digest* as a makeshift desk.

I have just checked the "no" boxes for bankruptcy filings, evictions, convictions, and "not paying rent," when a man's voice calls out my name. It's Richard Lee. Everything about him looks expensive, from his shoes to his haircut.

I stand up. "I'm Olivia Reinhart."

My name clearly means nothing to him, which is a relief. He stretches out his hand. "Richard Lee. Christina's on the phone, and everyone else is at lunch." He looks around, his forehead creasing. "So your family wants to rent the property? Your mom?"

"No. Just me." I hold out my application.

He doesn't reach for it. Instead, his smile vanishes like a magic trick. "Don't take this the wrong way, Olivia, but how old are you?"

"Seventeen, Richard, but I'm emancipated." I use his first name to let him know we're on the same level, two adults discussing a problem. "I've been renting an apartment in Portland, so I have a track record. And I'm transferring from the Burlingame Fred Meyer to the store down here."

"I'll be honest with you, because you seem like a nice kid. But you're still a kid. The last few years, the housing

74

market has been tough. I've taken chances on people who seemed nice, and I've gotten burned."

I try to sound calm. "Like I said, I have a job. And I've been paying rent for months with no problem." My Portland landlord is keeping my deposit, so he should still give me a good reference.

"As property managers, we're on the hook if someone skips out or trashes the place. And we only get a small percentage of the rent."

"Yes, but if a rental stays empty, any percentage of zero is still zero," I point out.

He continues as if he hasn't heard me. "And then when people can't make rent, they get roommates, so there's two or three times as much wear and tear for the same amount of money."

"It's just me. And it will stay just me. I promise."

"Do you know how many promises I hear? I'm sorry, but—"

I don't let him finish turning me down. "Okay, so the market's tough. And this house has already been sitting empty for months. With the murders back in the news, who's going to want to rent it now?"

He flinches a little. "You know about what happened?"

"Who doesn't?" I stretch the truth a little. "It's the first thing I heard when I stopped by to look at the house."

Even though there's no one else in the lobby, he looks around. "Come on back and let's talk about it."

I follow him down a hall. His office has a view of the valley through floor-to-ceiling windows. I sit in one of the visitor chairs in front of his desk.

"Nobody died at that house." Richard smooths the front of his elegant suit as he sits. "Those deaths happened miles away." On the polished expanse of his desk, there's just a sleek silver laptop and a penholder made of a can covered in burlap and lumpy felt flowers.

He must be a father, which for some reason surprises me. Something twists in my chest as I remember a series of school craft projects we were supposed to bring home to our parents, or at least our moms. First I gave them to Grandma. Later I sometimes handed them over to a foster mom. More often I stuffed them in the trash on my way out of school.

I force myself to persist. "Still, it's super creepy. Plus I heard that that lady's mom really *did* die there. Right in the kitchen." I push away the heartbreak of finding my grandma dead, turn it into the horror it would be for a stranger. "Who wants to live in a place associated with so much death?"

He closes his eyes for a second. "Look, I was good friends with the people who were killed. Especially Terry. So they're not just dead people to me." He focuses on me again. "They're not just *gossip*."

"I'm sorry," I say, but I can't let it rest, not when he might know something. "Why do *you* think they were killed?"

His words are low, as if pitched for his own ears. "Maybe they were just in the wrong place at the wrong time." He is quiet for a long time, then nods his head. "I'm going to take a chance on you, Olivia, but don't make me sorry."

I start to grin.

Then he says, "The rent is eight fifty a month. I'll just need first and last. We can take a credit or debit card or a check, although we'll need two days for it to clear." He looks at me expectantly, clearly waiting for me to fall to my knees in gratitude and then whip out my wallet.

The house is now slipping from my grasp. In my bank account, there's a little more than a thousand. "Could I make a down payment and then pay you the rest over a couple of weeks?" After all, I'll get it back. Eventually. Minus his company's 7 percent management fee.

His voice sharpens. "What? No. That's not how this works. Don't tell me how much you want to live there unless you also have the money to pay for it." His features pinch together. "I have a perfectly nice studio apartment I could probably get you into. It's six fifty a month. Why do you need a whole house?"

"I don't want to live in an apartment anymore. Do you know what it's like to be surrounded by other people all the time?" Look at this office, at his suit that probably cost more than my car. He can't know what it's like to hear everyone's arguments and flushing toilets. "Now I want some privacy. And no one's going to want to rent that house right now, not with the news, not when there are so many other rentals. The longer that house stays empty, the worse it will look. But if you let me rent it, I promise I'll take care of it. I'll make it look like a home again."

After a full minute of silence, he says, "As you point out, the house does need some sprucing up. I could let you paint the interior in exchange for the last month's rent. But it has to be a careful job or the deal's off. And I would need you to sign an agreement to that effect."

"Okay. You've got a deal."

Richard tilts his head and looks at me more closely. "Sure you don't want to go into the real estate business, Olivia? Because your talents are wasted at Fred Meyer."

CHAPTER 16

TURN THE KEY

FOR I DON'T KNOW HOW LONG, I'VE BEEN standing motionless on the front porch of what used to be my house and now is again. The key Richard gave me is in the lock, but I haven't turned it. Instead, I'm pinching it so hard it's leaving dents on the ball of my thumb and the side of my finger.

I can't let go, but at the same time I can't turn it. Am I ready to walk back in time? A sound makes me jump. It's my phone. I pull it from my pocket.

"Hello?"

"Exactly when were you planning on telling me you were leaving?"

My stomach does a flip. It's Bill. My boss in Portland. I was so nervous about going to Lee Realty I forgot all about needing to call him before Chuck did.

"Sorry!" I say. "Sorry, sorry, sorry."

"Why in the world would you want to live in Medford? You know what they call it. Dead-ford. Meth-ford."

Meth. Could my parents have been into drugs? "I just felt like I needed a change."

"Then dye your hair or get your belly button pierced or something. But don't move away and leave me short-handed." Bill's always been blunt. So if he was really mad at me, he would tell me. But still, there's some emotion under his words.

"I'm really sorry," I say again. "I was visiting a friend down here, and I just decided I liked it. It wasn't anything I planned."

"There are a million other places I would pick ahead of Medford. Bunch of rednecks in a little valley with a bad economy."

Bill begins listing all the reasons why no sane person would live in Medford, and as he does, I put my hand back on the key. Only this time I turn it, push the door open, and step through. My breath is stuck inside me, not coming in, not going out, as his litany continues. The lack of big-city culture. Smoky forest fires. Californians who have abandoned their own state for ours. Unbearable heat in the summer. Fog as thick as cotton in the winter.

As I walk into the living room, I'm prepared to be overwhelmed by memories, but the first hit I get is— nothing. Nothing about this place is familiar. There's a gold velour couch in the living room, but no other furniture on the flat gray carpet, just dents where it used to be. The walls are painted off-white. At least they were years ago. Shadowy rectangles of various sizes show where pictures have been put up and taken back down again. Cobwebs hang in the corners. It smells faintly of fried onions and dust.

"I'm not saying it's forever," I tell Bill. My shirt sticks to my skin. I pluck it away from my chest and let out a puff of air, finally able to breathe. "It's just for now. It's kind of hard to explain."

His voice loses some of its sarcastic humor. "Has someone on staff been giving you grief?"

Does Bill think I've come down here to get away from some harasser or a relationship gone wrong? "It's nothing like that." I turn sideways to maneuver through the small dining room, with its scarred wooden table and rickety chairs. "And who knows? I could come back."

"And why would I want someone who might quit at any time, with no notice?" Bill's teasing again. I think. Teasing with an edge, as he always does. "I told that Chuck guy you were a good worker but that you're leaving me in the lurch."

Have I just thrown away my life for nothing? Burned my bridges with Bill for a job I might not even get now?

"I'm sorry. It's just something that feels right." It takes only four strides to cross the narrow length of the kitchen. At the back is a tiny alcove just big enough to hold a washer and dryer, with a door to the backyard. I look through the glass pane at the yellowing lawn bordered by a fence on the far side and laurel hedges on the others.

He relents a little. "Don't worry. I didn't tell Chuck that last part. In fact, I pretty much talked him into hiring you."

"Thank you." I press my forehead against the cool glass as I try to imagine playing out there. But still I recognize nothing. "I really appreciate it."

"Let me know if you come to your senses and want

to head back here," Bill says. "And if you ever feel like telling me why you're there, you know how to get hold of me."

"Thanks. That means a lot to me." Especially now, when I'm starting to think I've made a big mistake.

After an awkward pause, we fumble through our good-byes.

On hollow legs, I retrace my steps and go down the hall. There's a single bathroom and three bedrooms. The one on the left is the biggest, but all of them are small, barely big enough for the beds they hold. Two rooms each have a twin bed, and the bigger one has a queen. They all have the same gray carpet, faintly stained in places. I think the carpet wasn't here when I was, but I can't be sure about that.

There's no magic. No memories. No flashbacks. I lived here the longest of any place I've ever lived, spent the first seven years of my life here, but it feels like a stranger's home. Nothing leads me back to my old self, my old family, to the dead who once walked through these rooms.

As I head back down the hall, tears close my throat. I was crazy to do this. Crazy to think this would jostle loose my memories. I reach out and touch the wall, steady myself.

Then I notice marks under my fingers. Faint pencil lines. They start at about midthigh and stop at about my chest. Next to each one is a bit of spidery writing, so light I can't really make it out.

But I know what the writing says. Each line has a date written next to it.

I close my eyes and put my heels against the wall.

Stand straight and tall, lengthening my spine as if it's an elastic cord. I can almost feel the pencil parting my hair as it pushes through to mark my height.

When I open my eyes, I see the cream-colored curtains behind the living room couch. Now I remember hiding behind them while Grandma pretended not to be able to find me. In the far corner of the living room is the spot where we always put up the Christmas tree. On that corner shelf in the dining room, there used to be a fat blue teapot.

Everything looks so much smaller and shabbier than I remember. But at least now I'm remembering, or whatever you call a feeling caught between dreaming and déjà vu.

Through the living room window, I see a guy skateboarding down the street. When he sees my car in the driveway, he stops, kicks the board up into his hands, and starts up the walk.

Duncan.

CHAPTER 17

BROKEN-OPEN INFINITY

I STEP OUT ON THE PORCH AS DUNCAN comes up the walk, his board tucked under his arm. He's wearing a red sleeveless T-shirt, jeans hacked off at the knees, and no helmet. His arms are muscled, and he has a scab on one tanned knee.

"Is this place all yours now?" he asks.

For an answer, I hold up the key. "And I think I got a job at Fred Meyer."

"Freddy's? That's where my mom works. In the garden center."

Crap. Chuck knows I'm from Portland. What if he tells the other staff that? Why did I tell Duncan I was from Seattle? Maybe I can think of a new lie that covers both the old lie and the real truth.

"Were your parents at the funeral?" I can't remember who he was sitting with.

"They were at work. My dad works for Glass Doctor. But they thought someone from our family should be there, and I didn't have to work on Saturday."

"Where do you work?"

"Zumiez. At the mall. Mostly I sell skateboards to kids and helmets to their moms." Medford is so small it has only one mall.

"And where's *your* helmet?" I'm the kind of person who always wears a seat belt or a bike helmet or work gloves. The world is full of too many risks without adding more.

"In my backpack." He gives me a half shrug. "I don't bother when I'm just street skating, like now. Only if I'm learning a trick. Or at the skate park. You have to wear a helmet there." His gaze flicks up to me. "Hey, can I ask you a weird question? Can I see your hand for a second? Your right hand?"

"Why?" Unconsciously, I put both hands behind my back.

"I was curious about that scar you have."

Slowly I put my hands in front of me, palms up. The scar is about a half inch long, near the base of my middle finger, a loop with two trailing ends. It looks like one of those ribbons people wear for breast cancer. Like a broken-open infinity sign.

All I really remember about it is having to get stitches. The doctor said they wouldn't hurt, but they did. That was before I figured out how often adults told you things they only wished were true.

"Do you remember how it happened?"

"No." Do I?

Gently, Duncan grasps my hand. My heart stutters in my chest. He touches the line with an index finger. "Do you remember who you were with?"

Something inside me freezes, like a mouse I once saw

on the floor of my apartment when I turned on the light. It didn't so much as twitch a whisker, as if I wouldn't notice it if it didn't move.

Feeling like I swallowed a stone, I look up from the scar to Duncan's steel-gray eyes. I pull my hands back and close them into fists.

"You were with me." His voice fills with urgency. "You're Ariel Benson."

I feel like I've been punched in the gut. "What? No!" Even though there's no one around, I keep my voice low. "I don't know what you're talking about."

"All afternoon, I've been riding my skateboard up and down this street, hoping I'd get a chance to talk to you." He pauses and then adds, "Ariel."

"I'm Olivia." I pat my chest. "Olivia Reinhart. Not this . . . this Ariel Benson. Because I'm not her." One of the times Tamsin took me to church, the pastor told the story of Peter, one of Jesus's disciples. Three times after Jesus's arrest, Peter was asked if he knew him, and three times he denied it.

"You may not remember how you got that scar, but I do. We were in first grade. I dared you to climb this big oak tree in our yard, and you lost your balance. You grabbed a branch on the way down, but it broke and cut your hand."

As Duncan says the words, I see them. Feel them. Relive the weightless tumble, my desperate reach, the bright pain that lanced across my palm. Remember how, when I landed flat on my back, the air was slammed out of my lungs.

He lets go of my hand and reaches for his back pocket.

"After I met you at the funeral, I came home and looked through boxes of old photos. I found this one of us." He pulls out a Polaroid and holds it up, his eyes going from me to the blond girl standing next to a dark-haired boy in the photo. Her face is no bigger than a thumbprint. I don't know how he can be so certain. It could be any blond little girl, and my hair is dark now. Duncan holds it out, but I don't take it. "You've changed a lot, but I remember that scar." He shakes his head, nearly smiling. "I got in so much trouble."

Steeling myself, I lift my chin. "I don't know how many times I have to tell you. My name is Olivia Reinhart. I can show you my driver's license."

He sets his jaw. "Maybe it is now, but that's not who you used to be." His voice softens. "What happened to you, Ariel?"

I blink so I won't cry. "I'm sorry, Duncan. But you're wrong. I'm not that poor little girl."

"How did you get that scar, then?" He lifts one eyebrow.

"From cooking." I cling to my lies, because what else do I have? "The knife slipped when I was making a stir-fry."

"Must have been some slip. Do you always hold things in the palm of your hand when you're trying to cut them?"

"Stop twisting everything around."

His eyes plead with me. "Why didn't you tell your family at the funeral? You're Terry's daughter. Terry and Naomi's. Carly and Tim and Lauren—they deserve to know. You're their niece, their cousin."

"Look, I don't know how many times I have to say

this: I'm Olivia Reinhart. I'm not Ariel Benson. I'm not. And please don't go telling people that I am." I won't admit the truth. I can't. But I come as close as I dare. "Don't you understand? This is my life you're talking about. You can't go around spreading rumors that are only going to cause people pain."

"Don't you think Terry's relatives have been in pain? Don't they deserve to be reunited with that little girl?" A muscle flickers in his jaw.

"Whoever she was, wherever she is, she's not here. Please, Duncan, don't go stirring up trouble where there isn't any. Can you promise me that you will keep this crazy idea to yourself? Please?" This might be the last time I ever talk to him. That thought hurts so much.

"All right, I'll keep your secret." He holds my gaze for one more bitter second. "But I don't have to like it." He spins on his heel and stalks off. Once he reaches the street, he throws down his board, jumps on, and is gone without a backward glance.

But it has to be this way. There's someone else out there who would be very interested in knowing who I am. The person who thought they got away with it. The person who killed my parents and then chose to drop me off at the Walmart.

Because maybe now they wouldn't be so generous.

CHAPTER 18

REACH INTO
THE DARK

I GO INSIDE, SIT ON THE SAGGING COUCH, and put my head in my hands. Tears prick my eyes. It's clear that Duncan and I can never be friends. Not now. I just dumped water on whatever spark was between us.

Is he right? Do I owe everyone the truth? Carly looked so sad at the funeral. And when I talked to Lauren in the bathroom, it felt like we could be friends.

But how can I figure out what really happened that day if people know who I am? They certainly won't tell me anything then. They won't let their guard down. Instead, they'll ask questions about what's happened in the past ten years. I don't feel like reciting my failures: the merry-go-round of foster-care placements, my broken relationship with Tamsin, my decision to leave school so I could escape the system.

Even Duncan looked at me differently when he thought I was from Seattle than he did when he realized I was the only surviving victim, the coda to a terrible story.

This house is the last place I was truly happy. I may

not remember my mom, but I do remember Grandma. Curling up together on the couch and watching TV. How I would ask what was for dinner and she would give me one teasing answer after another, no matter how I protested. "Tiger tails with daffodil sauce." "Fried tarantulas." "Barbecued unicorn horns." I would get so frustrated, stamping my foot and demanding to know the truth, even though I always ended up being a little disappointed when the real answer was Spanish rice or beef Stroganoff. She read to me every night before bed and praised every drawing I made. In her eyes, I was brilliant and beautiful.

I want to go back to that time, or at least make it look the same. The couch sits at a ninety-degree angle to the window. It's not the same couch, but I still get up and drag it until it sits with its back to the window—in the "right" place. Now I need to get a coffee table and a small TV to put in the built-in bookshelves, where ours used to sit.

The chairs in the dining room are different from the ones I remember, but close enough. I think the table is even the same table, much the worse for wear.

I go back down the hall and turn right into one of the small bedrooms. The bed is along one wall, but I use my knees to slowly push it across the carpet until it's underneath the window. Where it's supposed to be. My grandma across the hall, and my mom's room here, with my room on the other side. After my mom died, this room became a shrine. When I was growing up, her hairbrush still sat on a little table next to the bed, and her clothes hung in the closet.

But is everything gone? Moving like a sleepwalker,

I go over to the closet. It doesn't have a door anymore. Dropping to my knees, I fist my fingers in the nap of the gray carpet. I yank and pull at the far corner until, with a squeal of staples, the carpet peels free. I don't know what I'm doing; at least my mind doesn't, but my body does.

Underneath are pristine fir floorboards, unscarred, since no one ever walked in the corner of the closet. I stick my fingernail under the edge of one. It lifts up, revealing a space about ten inches wide and six inches deep.

Then I reach into the dark.

CHAPTER 19

BLACK AND WHITE

MY FINGERTIPS GRAZE SOMETHING. I GRAB it, then twist to pull it free.

It's an old cigar box. It used to be my mom's. Sometimes she would look at the things inside while I played on the floor.

I sit back on my heels, cradling the box to my chest. Now I have two new memories of my mom. In the cemetery I remembered her reading to me, and now this.

My grandma never knew about the box, and after my mom died, I didn't say anything. It was full of treasures and secrets, and she might have taken them away. On days when I was really sad, I would go into my mom's old room, shut the door, take out the box, and slowly sift through the contents.

My grandma respected that closed door. Sometimes she went into my mom's room herself, although I think she just lay on the bed and wept. Afterward, she would come out, her face still red and faintly damp, and give me a long hug.

I flip up the gold-colored clasp. Inside the lid, *Victory* is written in flowery red script. I spread the contents out on the floor. The things I liked as a kid don't hold as much interest for me now. A dollar bill folded into a ring, a pink-and-white spiral shell, thirteen wheat pennies, a ticket stub from a concert. When I pick up a dried corsage, the petals crumble at my touch. At the sight of a lock of fine blond hair tied with a pink ribbon, I feel my eyes get wet. It must be mine.

But none of these things seem like clues. And what I need is for my mom to have left some kind of sign. Evidence. A hidden message. Because the detective didn't think it could have been a stranger who stabbed her. Did my mom save a clue from the person who killed her and my dad?

I straighten out a piece of notebook paper that's been folded and unfolded so many times it's separating at the creases.

Please Naomi please just give me a chance to talk
to you. Whenever you want. Just please say yes.
Please.

It's not signed. Written by my dad or someone else? Whoever it was, they sounded desperate.

Could my mom have been killed because she didn't say yes?

Or because she did?

Underneath is an old valentine, the cheap kind kids give one another in grade school that come thirty to a pack. Penciled in tiny letters on the envelope is *Made, enveloped, and licked in China* next to a hand-drawn stamp. It's addressed to Naomi "I Moan" Benson. The humor seems a little too adult for grade school, but then I realize *I moan* is *Naomi* spelled backward. On the back flap, someone has written, *If your an infearior person to insults do not open this card.* Misspellings and questionable word usage aside, the card makes me smile. Inside the envelope is a cartoon bird wearing a red hat. Printed on the brim is *Valentine . . .* and in a heart around the bird's neck are the words *Be mine.*

On the back someone has written *Happy Valentine's Day. You cutie you.* It's signed, but not by my dad. I can only make out the first initial, but it's a *J.* Jason, the guy who talked about my dad at the funeral, his best friend?

I look at the handwriting on the pleading note. I'm not sure, but I don't think it's from the same person. Of course, handwriting changes as people get older, and the card's obviously from a kid, so I could be wrong. But all the *T*s in the first note look almost like capital letter *A*s, each with a tiny opening at the top where the pen went up and then went back down a fraction to the right before curling up at the end. The *T*s on the valentine are straight up and down.

Did my mom keep this card because it was sweet and funny? Or because it was a link to a feeling she hadn't left behind when she outgrew cheap paper valentines? Was there once something between my mom and the *J* person? Between her and Jason?

Maybe the next thing in the box holds the answer to that question. It's a wedding invitation that's been crumpled up and smoothed out, like she was going to throw it away and changed her mind. For Jason and Heather. My parents' best friends. I remember seeing Heather glare at him at the funeral, so I don't think they're together anymore. They'd gotten married about six months before my parents died.

Even if my mom had been upset about the wedding, even if she had feelings for Jason, how could that have led to her and my dad being murdered in the forest? If Jason didn't want to be with her, why would he kill her, let alone both of them?

His breathing had hitched when he talked about them. But maybe he wasn't sorry they were dead. Maybe he was worried he would get caught.

At the very bottom of the box are two strips of black-and-white photo-booth photos, four photos to a strip.

The first shows my mom and dad and Jason, recognizable because of his Hawaiian shirt. The two guys are crowded in on either side of my mom. In the first photo, my mom just looks amazingly beautiful, lips pursed in a pout, eyes wide, dark eyebrows like wings. Her face is turned toward my dad, but she only has eyes for the camera. The two guys are facing the camera, sticking out their tongues. Jason's eyes are closed.

The second photo is just a blur of motion. They must have been trying to change positions, but they didn't make it in time. The only thing I can clearly make out is someone's hand pressed against the curtain at the back of the booth.

In the third photo, everyone's grinning and making their hands like claws.

In the fourth, my mom seems to be sitting on Jason's lap while my dad leans in. They're all laughing. If there was ever something between my mom and Jason, did my dad know?

The next strip shows only my mom and dad. They're wearing different clothes, so it must have been a different day. Their foreheads are shiny, like maybe it was summer. My mom's wearing a chunky necklace, and her hair is pulled back on one side with a silver barrette. My dad's hair is messy, as if he hadn't combed it since he rolled out of bed.

In the first photo, they look a little formal, like this is the photo that proves they're a couple. In the second, he's turned toward her, his eyes nearly closed, as if he's getting ready to kiss her. She's not looking at him, but rather up and away. Maybe she didn't have enough time to purse her lips.

Or maybe she did.

In the third one, their funny faces make me smile. One of her eyes is closed, the other points toward her nose, and she's hooked her lower lip with her upper teeth. He's got one eyebrow raised, chin thrust forward, and his tongue so far out of his mouth that he looks like the weird logo for that old group the Rolling Stones.

I look down at the last photo in the strip and stop smiling.

My parents have put on terrorized looks, eyebrows raised, whites showing around their eyes, lips pulled back.

When these photos were taken, it was all just a game, no more real or serious than when they pretended to be monsters. Just having fun.

But this must be close to how my parents looked in the last few seconds of their lives.

What had it been like for my mom when the knife first cut her? The nineteenth time?

But now maybe she's left me some clues. I need to find out more about what happened between her and Jason. What happened between the three of them.

Because it might have something to do with why only one of them is still alive.

CHAPTER 20

WHAT THEY LEFT BEHIND

MEDFORD'S GOODWILL SMELLS THE SAME as any Goodwill—like dust, old shoes, musty books, and disinfectant. Still, the cool interior is a welcome relief. I grab a cart and start pushing it down the graying linoleum. One wheel squeaks.

Last night I ate from the McDonald's dollar menu, then slept on a bare mattress with only my arms for a pillow. My goal is to get the minimum and hope it comes to less than forty bucks. I need a set of sheets, a towel, and one each of the most basic kitchen things. Or maybe two, because I want to have Nora over, make her some of the foods she no longer can cook. I think of Duncan, of how I'll never be able to invite him over, and push the thought away. Chuck asked me to start work tomorrow, so I also need a white shirt to wear with my black pants, and maybe a few more summer clothes. Medford seems to run at least ten degrees hotter than Portland.

For the queen-size bed, I find sheets with different patterns and a pillowcase that doesn't match either sheet.

It takes a little longer to find a pillow that's unstained. I don't mind used, but I do have my standards.

The kitchen stuff is easier. There's a better selection, and some of the items, like two tumblers and a coffee cup, look brand-new.

I'm in the clothing section, holding a white peasant blouse against me to see if it fits, when someone says, "That's cute. You should get it."

It's the girl with the purple hair from the funeral. Lauren. My cousin, even though she doesn't know it. The girl Duncan said I was hurting by not telling the truth. Today she still has the rings in her nose and ear, but the silver chain connecting them is gone. Despite what she claimed during the argument with her mom, maybe the chain's purpose was to bug people.

"Thanks." The blouse is $2.99. After a second, I put it in the cart.

"We talked at the funeral," she says. "My name's Lauren."

"I'm Olivia." I pick up a pair of cutoffs, not meeting her eyes. What if she recognizes me, the way Duncan did? I'm careful to keep my fingers curled over my scar.

"How did you know my uncle?"

"I didn't. I just moved in next door to Nora Murdoch. She asked me to drive her because she wasn't feeling well."

"I know that house. It's cute. That's where my uncle's girlfriend grew up." She pulls a red sleeveless shirt over the black tank top she's wearing.

Medford's small enough that everyone knows everything, I guess. Except who killed my parents. I realize I should say something.

"I'm, uh, sorry for your loss."

Her brows draw together for a second. "What? Oh, my uncle? I only remember him and his girlfriend a little bit." So much for her suffering, the way Duncan said. "My family spent years *not* talking about Uncle Terry because most of them secretly thought he was a killer." She takes off the shirt and puts it in her shopping basket. "My mom used to wonder if the cops were monitoring our mail or phone calls. Sometimes she even thought Terry did it."

"So was her brother, like, abusive to his girlfriend?" I hold my breath. I don't want to know, but I need to.

She shakes her head. "I don't think so." Her bangs fall back into their perfect straight line above her eyes. "Maybe my mom just figured you can never really know what someone is capable of."

"So *now* who does she think did it?"

"I think she's hoping it was a stranger. Some drifter who was just passing through, left my uncle's car in Portland and kept on going. Maybe went on to the next town or the next state and found some more people to kill."

"Why is she hoping that?"

"If it was someone here who did it, it would probably be a person she knew. Maybe even a friend."

A lot of people in this town probably feel the same. Maybe they think what happened was long ago, that it's time to forget and move on. Especially if the truth is going to add more pain, rip open the old wound and make it even deeper.

"I heard that guy Jason used to have a crush on Naomi," I say.

Her eyes open wider. "Who told you that?"

"Someone was talking at the funeral."

Lauren thinks about this. "He's kind of a weird dude. Everything about him is loud—how he talks, those Hawaiian shirts. And he always thinks there's some conspiracy or something. He used to be married to Heather, who was Naomi's best friend. My mom says it's not easy being married to a trucker, because they're gone all the time." She shrugs. "Still, even if he had a crush on Naomi, why would he kill her, too?"

I don't have a good answer for that.

We're at the registers now. Lauren falls in behind me. "So you're living on your own?" she asks, eyeing my cart.

"Yeah. I'm saving for college, and the cost of living is cheaper here."

"I'm going to U of O, but it's impossible to find a job in Eugene over the summer, so I had to come home. You know what they say: Home's the place where when you have to go there, they have to take you in."

My total comes to $22.35. When we go outside, it's so hot it doesn't feel quite real.

"Want to go to Grocery Outlet?" Lauren points at the store across the parking lot.

"I've never been in one," I say, then wonder if there are any in Seattle, my supposed hometown. I've heard the food at Grocery Outlet is really cheap. When you work at Freddy's, there's an unspoken rule you will never be caught by a customer, even in your off-hours, in Safeway, Albertsons, or another competitor. But while I'm still anonymous, I'm free to shop where I want.

"It's, like, the cheapest store in the world." She laughs. "My dad calls it the Island of Misfit Food."

As we go up and down the aisles, Lauren's dad's comment starts to make sense. I see crackers that look like Wheat Thins but with Spanish labels. Flavors and colors of Gatorade I've never seen before. The cheese selection in the cold case is kind of random, but there's some good stuff here, like Brie, aged Cheddar, and goat cheese, all going for about half of what Fred Meyer charges.

Grocery Outlet also seems to be where food flops go to die, and we take turns pointing them out. Pork Helper instead of Hamburger Helper. Canned egg salad. Shelf-stable salmon pie. It's like an alternate reality. As if aliens made a grocery store to fool us, only they didn't get the details right. The thought makes me stop in my tracks.

Lauren bumps into me. "Olivia?"

I don't answer. Whoever killed my parents must have tried to tell a story with what they left behind. Maybe they hid my dad's body so he would be blamed. And then left his car at the airport so it looked like he took off. But that story was a lie. The cops were too focused on my dad to ask why he had bothered to wipe his prints off his *own* truck. There must be other ways the killer slipped up, made a mistake, screwed up the details.

Maybe I can figure out where they went wrong.

CHAPTER 21

THAT GIRL DOESN'T EXIST

'M NEARING THE END OF MY FIRST DAY AT Freddy's when I hear something falling on the black rubber mat behind me. A lot of somethings. When I turn, half the pyramid of Granny Smiths I had just stacked is gone. Duncan stands next to it, red-faced. He puts down his basket and skateboard and starts picking up the scattered apples.

My heart speeds up. Abandoning my produce cart, I stalk over.

He looks up. "Sorry. I guess I made an apple-lanche."

Even though his pun is pretty good, I ignore it. I ignore his strong jaw, muscled arms, and beautiful eyes. My heart is reacting one way, but my head has to be in charge. "What are you doing here?"

"Buying groceries." Still on his knees, he begins gathering apples.

"I'm sure your mom can take care of that for you, since she *works* here." With the toe of one of my Vans, I kick an apple toward him.

The flush deepens. "I've been thinking about what you said." His voice is urgent and low. "And about why you might have said it. I want to help you."

I look around. There's no one near us. "You want to help me?"

"Yeah. I do." He cradles a half dozen apples.

"Then leave me alone!"

Duncan's unfazed. "That's why you moved down here, isn't it? To figure out who did it?" He gets to his feet and starts fitting the apples into empty spaces, one by one.

It's clear I don't have any other choice but to talk to him. Or at least give him a talking-to. I huff a sigh. "Do you know where the employees park their cars?" When he nods, I say, "I'm off in fifteen minutes. Meet me back there."

Pushing my produce cart through the black rubber swinging doors that lead to the prep room, I spend the last few minutes of my day grinding my teeth as I cut and wrap watermelon chunks. When I go out to the parking lot, Duncan's doing kickflips next to my car. He's still not wearing a helmet, so he must think he's got this trick down. As I watch, he steps on the board wrong and almost takes a header. For some reason, his near miss makes me even madder.

"Get in." I unlock his door and then mine.

It's like crawling into an oven. But I don't need anyone to overhear what I've got to say. "This is my life." I shake my finger in his face. "And I don't need you to go messing it up by spreading crazy rumors."

"You're right. It *is* your life. I wasn't thinking it through, and I'm really sorry. After I left, I realized it's about more than just Carly and Lauren, isn't it? Because they aren't the only ones who'd want to know that you've come back to Medford. Whoever killed your parents would probably be very interested in finding out what you remember." He takes my right hand. I'm so surprised I don't pull it back. He runs his thumb across my scar, and even in the heat, a shiver dances across my skin.

I pull my hand back. Push my feelings away. "So who else knows that Ariel had a scar?" I tried dabbing foundation on my palm this morning, but it lasted only a few minutes under the prep sink.

"Maybe my parents?" He shrugs. "But they might not remember the specifics. Maybe just me, since I'm the one who got in so much trouble for daring you."

"There's something you need to understand. My name is Olivia Reinhart now. Ariel Benson—that girl doesn't exist anymore. But that doesn't mean she doesn't matter. That doesn't mean she doesn't deserve justice, or that her parents don't deserve justice. And I'm the only one who can give it to her."

"Okay." Duncan nods. "I hear you. But you can't do it all by yourself. You're going to need someone to help you find out what really happened."

My guard goes right back up. "This isn't any of your business."

"Maybe you don't think it is, but you should still let me help. Because if you're the only one asking questions, people are going to notice and start asking questions themselves. But me—they'll just think I'm curious. They won't worry that I have an ulterior motive. And who else knows this town better than someone who's lived here their whole life?"

No matter how much I want to do this by myself, Duncan's words make a lot of sense.

He must see my hesitation. "I never forgot you. Is it so wrong for me to want to help an old friend?"

"Okay, you want to help?" I turn the ignition. "Then let's get started."

CHAPTER 22

MORE VICTIMS

"SO *DO* YOU REMEMBER ANYTHING ABOUT that day?" Duncan asks as I drive us back to my house.

"If you had asked me last week, I would have said I didn't remember anything." I sigh. "Not about what happened that day or anything before it. I didn't even really remember my parents. But ever since I came back to Medford, I've been having these little flashes."

"Of what?" Duncan looks half-curious, half-horrified.

"Once it was of being in a snowy forest. I think that must have been when we had just started looking for the Christmas tree. And I can remember my mom reading to me. I even remembered where she hid a box of keepsakes." Did I do the same thing, tuck away my memories, even from myself? "And after the memorial, I dreamed about seeing a bloody knife lying on the floor of a car." My scalp prickles just thinking about it.

"Oh my God." Duncan turns in his seat to me, his gray eyes wide. He echoes my thoughts. "Maybe everything that happened that day is still all there, inside your head."

"If it is, I wish I could figure out how to get it out. I don't want to just wait around for a dream or some random phrase to make me remember. I want to know now."

Duncan doesn't respond, just takes his phone out of his pocket. He starts tapping on it. The car is quiet for the remaining few minutes it takes me to drive home. What am I doing, spilling my deepest secrets to a stranger who isn't really even paying attention?

"Hypnosis," he says as I pull into my driveway.

"What?" I turn off the car.

"Maybe hypnosis could help." He hands over his phone.

He's pulled up an old news story from 1976. In Chowchilla, California, twenty-six children and their bus driver were kidnapped and locked in a moving van that had been buried in a gravel quarry. After they managed to escape, a hypnotist put the bus driver under, and he remembered the license plate number of one kidnapper's car.

But when I think of hypnotists, I think of country fairs or weight-loss ads. Not crime solving. I hand his phone back. "But that was a fresh memory. Mine's nearly fourteen years old. And I was only three when it happened."

Duncan looks hurt. "It might be worth a try."

When we go inside, I point at the couch. "Wait here. I'm going to get something." I walk down the hall and come back with my mom's cigar box. I hand it to him.

"What is this?" he asks before he opens it.

"It belonged to my mom. It's got all her keepsakes. She used to hide it under the floorboards of her closet."

His eyebrows go up. "You mean—here? In this house?"

"Yeah. It's been here all along. I think I was the only one who knew about it, besides my mom. My grandma didn't know."

When he flips back the lid, right on top is the Halloween photo, the one I took from the bulletin board at the service. I had put it in the box along with my dad's program, never thinking anyone else would look at these things.

He picks it up. "Hey, I remember seeing this picture at the memorial. You have a copy, too, huh?"

"Um, I took it."

He jerks his head back. "What?"

"I don't have any photos of just my dad or even of my family. I think my grandma threw away any photo with my dad in it after my mom's body was found. And she never talked about him."

His eyebrows pull together. "But—that was someone's photo."

Guilt pinches me. I ignore it. "Yeah, it was. But whoever put it up probably has lots of photos of my dad. I've got nothing."

Duncan doesn't say anything more, though the way he twists his mouth, he doesn't have to.

I set the photo and the program aside and show him the begging note. "Have you ever seen that handwriting before?"

He purses his lips. "I don't think so."

"I don't think it's Jason's, unless it really changed." I unearth the old valentine and watch Duncan smile as he reads the childish insults. "But I do wonder about Jason. Look at this invitation to his wedding to Heather." I pull it out. "Why would my mom crumple it up unless she still had feelings for him?"

"Wait." He holds up a hand. "So you're thinking *Jason* might have killed your parents?"

"The cops told me that the first person they would have looked at would have been a lover. And I'm pretty sure there was something between them at some point."

"Look, you're talking about Jason. That guy's just a blowhard. Not a killer."

"Then what about Sam? It's clear she was in love with my dad. You saw how she cried over him at the funeral. Maybe those were really tears of guilt."

"Sam?" Duncan makes a face. "She's as thin as a straw. I mean, she seems pretty tightly wound, but I can't see her hurting someone."

"In Portland, the detective told me it could have been a woman, if she was motivated by some strong emotion, like hatred or even panic."

Duncan shakes his head. "Hey, look, I've known Jason and Sam since I was a kid. And they're not killers. Do you really think one of them snapped fourteen years ago and then just went back to being normal?"

Why did I ever say yes to him? He may be cute, but he's so nice that he can't believe other people could be not so nice. "Then what do *you* think happened?"

"I think your mom and dad must have crossed paths with a serial killer. Some crazy guy in the woods."

"Serial killer implies a *series* of murders. If it was a serial killer, then why weren't there more victims?"

"Maybe there were." Duncan picks up his backpack. "Last night I was trying to figure out what happened. It turns out there are websites that keep track of unsolved murders. You can sort them by year or geographic area. So look at this." He hands me a printout showing a girl with long dark hair parted down the middle. "This is Angie Paginini. She lived in Grants Pass." Grants Pass is about a half hour away. "A year after your parents died, she left her high school play rehearsal, but she never made it home. Two days later, her body was found in a park—a *wooded* park. She had been stabbed to death. She even looks like your mom."

I regard the photo critically. Maybe. Or maybe they only look alike because they're both girls from the same time period with the same hair color. All I say is, "But it wasn't just my mom who died. It was both my parents."

"That's happened before, too." He slips another piece of paper into my hands. "Six months before your parents died, another couple in their twenties was killed in Northern California. Shot to death in their sleeping bags. Right on the beach. No sexual assault, no robbery, no known motive, and no suspects. Just like your parents."

Medford's only thirty minutes from the California border. But it's a much longer drive to the coast. And— "That was a gun, though. Not a knife."

"Nobody knows how your dad was killed," Duncan points out. "And I was reading that serial killers will sometimes just use whatever's available."

"It's hard to believe that my parents were killed by some random stranger. I mean, why would a serial killer murder them and then let me live? But if it was someone my family knew, they might have felt a connection to me."

"Serial killers don't murder every single person they

111

come across." Duncan's eyes look stormy. "They pick their targets. Maybe your parents fit and you didn't."

Or maybe Duncan just doesn't want to believe it could be someone he knows.

I think of foster homes where I lived in fear but smiled for the caseworker. Or where the house was a pigsty unless a visit was scheduled. If I've learned anything in the past ten years, it's that a lot of people have one face in public and another in private.

CHAPTER 23

BEST FRIENDS

I BOUNCE FROM FOOT TO FOOT AS I WAIT for Duncan in the Medford Public Library reference room. Our plan was to start by researching what happened back then, but now I've got something even more interesting to tell him.

"You're not the only one who can Google," I say in a low voice as soon as he walks in.

"What do you mean?" He looks wary. He's keeping his voice quiet, too, even though we're the only ones in the room.

We're standing so close together that I can feel the heat of his body, but I don't let myself think about that. Instead, I say, "Did you know there's one job that the FBI thinks is so linked to serial killers that they've created a whole task force for it?" Still buzzing with what I read online last night, I don't wait for him to answer. "Long-haul truckers." *Just like Jason.*

"Truckers?"

"The FBI thinks that serial killers who work as

long-haul truckers have killed more than *five hundred* hitchhikers, hookers, and people whose cars have broken down. They say it's the perfect cover for a serial killer. Truckers work by themselves, and they're always on the move. They can pick up a victim in one state, kill them in another, and dump their body in a third."

"But they're talking about truckers who kill strangers." Duncan doesn't sound nearly as confident as he did last night "Not people they know. Not their best friends. So that would rule out Jason."

"Maybe my parents were the start." I drop my voice to a near-soundless whisper. "Maybe Jason killed them and then got a taste for killing."

His mouth twists. "Thousands of people are truckers. Probably hundreds of thousands. Just because a few are serial killers doesn't mean they all are. All squares are rectangles, but not all rectangles are squares."

Duncan liked the idea of a serial killer when he thought that meant it couldn't be anyone he knew. "All I'm saying is we need to look at Jason more closely."

He finally nods. Reluctantly.

When I asked the librarian earlier, she told me the reference room had copies of all the high school annuals, one for each year. Now I find the section, then the annuals for North Medford and the year my parents graduated. I open it to the index. With Duncan leaning in, I run my finger down a column of tiny type. *Badger, Barrett, Beckstrom.*

Benson, Naomi. My mom's name is followed by a series of page numbers: 132, 244, 248, 273. I have only one photo of my mom, but this annual has *four*.

I turn to page 132. And there's my mom. It's one of those first-day-of-school photos, the ones the photo vendor tries to sell you sets of. None of my foster families ever bought them, not even the cheapest package with eight wallet-size shots.

Duncan says, "She's really pretty."

My mom wears a black top with a scoop neck. Her wavy brown hair falls past her shoulders. Her large dark eyes are focused on something to her right. Her lips are pursed, making her look either dubious or uncertain. I wonder what she was thinking.

On page 244 is a photo of the choir, dozens of people dressed in identical red robes. If my mom wasn't identified as being in the third row (*N. Benson*), I don't think I would be able to pick out her tiny dot of a face.

Page 248 reveals she was also in the National Honor Society. So she was smart. About two dozen people pose in front of an oak tree. My mom sits cross-legged in the first row. She wears jeans and a cream-colored cardigan with a shawl collar. Her smile is so wide her eyes are nearly closed. I lightly run my thumb over her face. A bubble expands in my chest, crowding my lungs.

Page 273 has the annual's only photo of my parents together. They're part of a crowd at a cafeteria table, all of them raising their milk cartons and juice bottles as if toasting the photographer. It's easy to pick out my parents. Not only are they in the middle of the photo, but they look exactly as I expect them to. They never had a chance to change.

Duncan points. "Hey, that's gotta be Jason." Even back then, he was wearing a Hawaiian shirt, but his face was fuller, his arms thicker.

"And check out who he's looking at," I point out. "My mom. Not the camera. Not Heather"—she's sitting next to my mom—"even though that's who he ended up marrying."

The woman sitting on the other side of my dad looks familiar. Wide cheekbones, blond hair—it's Sam, with longer hair. She's half-turned toward my dad. He's sitting between her and my mom, but he's grinning at the camera.

"Who's that?" Duncan taps on a guy sitting next to Sam.

If he wasn't the only Asian-looking guy at the table, I wouldn't recognize him. He wears a faded T-shirt, and his hair hangs raggedly in his eyes. "That's Richard Lee. You know, the real estate guy."

The only one I don't recognize is a guy with close-cropped orange-red hair who is sitting at the end of the table. " 'Ben Gault,' " I read aloud from the caption. "Do you know him?"

"I don't think so. Maybe he moved away."

In the back of the annual, there are only two page numbers next to *Terry Weeks:* one for his yearbook portrait, the other for the photo in the cafeteria. I guess the kinds of things my dad liked—concerts and parties, hanging out at the river, driving a Trans Am too fast—aren't the activities that make it into the annual. He wasn't on a team; he wasn't in a play; he didn't sing in the choir.

I make photocopies of everything, and then Duncan puts the annual away. I go back to the librarian at the information desk. "Do you have old copies of the *Medford Mail Tribune?*"

"How far back do you want to go?" Her dark hair is cut in curly points that frame her face. "We have paper copies for the last year. Anything older than that is on microfiche."

"About fourteen years ago."

She presses her lips together and looks at us more closely. "First you wanted to look at annuals and now old newspapers. Is this about Terry Weeks and Naomi Benson?"

Duncan and I exchange glances, and then I nod. My cheeks are on fire.

"Everyone's asking about them," she says. "I was a couple of years behind them in high school. Terry Weeks was really cute. Not that he noticed me."

Duncan asks, "Do *you* have any theories about what happened?"

"Maybe they picked up a hitchhiker, but he was crazy."

I try to imagine it. A confrontation that turned ugly but stopped short of killing a kid.

She finds the right film and threads it through the reader. The machine looks like one of those old boxy computers you see in movies, as deep as they are tall.

I turn the knob, and time flickers by. Since my mom (and my dad, too, although no one knew it) died near the end of the year, there are a lot of pages to go through.

It still seems likely to me that they were killed by someone they knew.

But could Duncan and the librarian be right, that it was a stranger? A serial killer who didn't know them? A deranged hitchhiker? Or someone who targeted them for a different reason?

The cops said my parents didn't have anything to steal, but I realize that someone could still have killed them for the pickup. Once pictures of the truck were shown on *America's Most Wanted*, the killer might have figured it was too hot and dumped it. After all, just because the pickup was found at the airport's long-term lot weeks after the murders doesn't mean it was there the whole time.

The newspaper images are still spooling by when I grunt as if someone just hit me in the stomach. My gut knew what I saw faster than my thumb and fingers did.

"What is it?" Duncan leans in.

I scroll back. It's a photo I haven't seen before, captioned "Family Missing." My dad wears a baseball cap and a light-colored T-shirt. He grips a can of beer in his right hand. His left arm is around my mom's slender waist. She's wearing a dark short-sleeved shirt with contrasting trim. Her hand is on her hip, a stack of bracelets on her wrist. It must be summer, because I'm standing in front of them wearing a sleeveless top, my blond hair falling past my shoulders. My head isn't even as high as their waists.

The story starts out as front-page news. Each succeeding day, it gets smaller and moves further inside the paper. None of the information is new to me.

And then I read a paragraph that makes my stomach cram itself into the back of my throat.

Several times, police have been called to the house Naomi Benson and her daughter shared with Benson's mother, to deal with fights between Benson and Weeks. Medford Police Department files show that Weeks was under a Nov. 26 temporary restraining order forbidding him from coming within 100 yards of Benson after a domestic-violence complaint was filed. However, police have also said Benson willingly went with Weeks to look for a Christmas tree.

Duncan looks at me wide-eyed. I feel as if I'm being wrenched back and forth. My dad was guilty, my dad was innocent. Now he sounds guilty again.

I grab Duncan's arm as a new idea takes root. "What if my dad really did it?"

CHAPTER 24

THE TRUTH

AN OLD WOMAN SITTING AT A NEARBY computer furrows her brow and puts her finger to her lips.

I drop my voice to a whisper. "What if my dad really did kill my mom? And then killed himself?" In my mind's eye, I see how it could have played out. Have we been looking at everything the wrong way? Nausea rises in me. I swallow back the bitterness.

"What if there was another person there that day, like the librarian said?" I ask Duncan. "Maybe a hitchhiker or even a friend?"

I imagine my dad having yet another fight with my mom. Only this time it turned deadly. Meanwhile, the third adult stood by, too horrified or too afraid to act. Or maybe they ran into the woods. I picture them creeping back to find my mom dead, my dad dying from a self-inflicted wound, me the only survivor.

"Maybe they couldn't stop what was happening, and

afterward they were too afraid to deal with cops," I go on. What if they had an arrest record or had simply been too anxious to face the questions? "They could have figured the Walmart was a safe place to drop me, and then left the car at the airport, wiped it down, and went on their way."

I squeeze Duncan's arm so tight he grimaces. I've been feeling sorry for my dad, for misjudging him all these years. But maybe I was wrong.

"No." Duncan shakes himself free. "Wait a minute. That was a pickup your family was in. I don't think there would be room for another person."

Duncan's right. Or at least probably right. There's nothing to say that I didn't end up on someone's lap. But it's a less likely scenario.

"Chief Spaulding said they were reopening the case," he continues. "There still could be evidence that they never got around to testing back when they figured they didn't need to, because they thought your dad did it. There must have been footprints or even tire tracks."

Now he's the one who's imagining things that probably aren't true.

"Yeah, but it was three weeks before those grouse hunters found my mom's body," I point out. "There would have been a lot more snow in between." I see that little flash of memory again, the blanket of white lying untouched underneath the trees. I've always loved how snow makes everything new, but in this case it helped hide the truth.

"There still could be other clues," Duncan insists. "Fingerprints on that tarp or maybe on the clothes your mother was wearing. DNA where the killer touched. Maybe blood, if the killer got cut swinging around that knife. Fibers from the killer's clothing."

A surge of hope pulses through me. The police must be testing things right now. Running them under special lights, picking up pieces of hair with tweezers. The truth of what happened that day might be answered in a lab.

CHAPTER 25

RAINING BLOOD

I DON'T KNOW WHERE I EXPECTED A HYPNOTIST to have an office, but I'm pretty sure it wasn't right next to a Paradise Tans in a strip mall. Duncan wanted to go with me, but he was scheduled to work at the same time as the first open appointment time she had. Besides, I'm not nearly as certain as he is that this plan will work. I take a deep breath and open the door.

The woman sitting behind the desk unfolds herself and gets to her feet. Tall and slender, she has bright blue eyes and close-cropped hair bleached white-blond. She's nothing like I was expecting.

"Are you Quinn Columbo?" I ask.

She nods. "You must be Olivia."

"That's right." We shake hands. Like the rest of her, her fingers are long and thin.

She half sits on the edge of her desk. "On the phone you said you're interested in being hypnotized?"

"Maybe." I resist the sudden urge to leave. "First, I want to know more about how it works."

"Of course. People sometimes think hypnosis is something unfamiliar and scary. But you've actually been in hypnotic states before. We all have. Like when you get so lost in a book or a movie that you don't notice anything else around you. That's a hypnotic state. Or when you're driving and suddenly you're at your exit, only you don't remember how you got there."

I nod, thinking of my drive to Medford, how I lost track of long stretches of freeway while thinking about my parents.

"Hypnosis is a state of hyperfocus." She bunches her fingers and taps them together. "It's not sleeping and it's not unconsciousness. You're fully awake. But because your attention is so focused, you have less peripheral awareness." She pulls her fingers apart, wiggling them in all directions.

What she's saying makes sense, but I'm still hesitant. "Once at the county fair I saw a hypnotist tell a guy he was a dog. He got on all fours and started barking." He scurried around the small wooden stage, his tongue hanging out, while his friends in the audience fell over with laughter. "You won't make me do anything like that, will you?"

Quinn frowns. "People who volunteer want to be in the spotlight. They already know they'll be asked to do silly things, so they accept the hypnotist's suggestions."

But what about not-so-silly things? "Could you hypnotize a person to do something bad? Like commit a murder or something?"

"What! No. Not if it was something they would never do." She leans forward. "So what is it you want to work on today?"

"There's something else I have to ask you first."

"Okay." She tilts her head and waits.

"If I tell you something, does it stay here in this room? Just between us?"

"I'm bound by our code of ethics to respect confidentiality. So, yes, what you tell me stays here. The only exception would be if you were a danger to yourself, or if you were threatening to harm someone. Or if I were subpoenaed by a judge."

This last exception gives me pause. Right now, who I am is a secret. And I want it to stay that way.

Quinn must see my expression. "Let me just say that in my twenty years in the business, that's never happened." She takes a slow breath. Everything about her is unhurried. "Hypnotherapy is a tool. It can help you lose weight, or stop smoking, or realize something about yourself." Her gaze is direct. "What are you hoping to do?"

"I want"—I have to swallow before I can say anything more—"I want to remember something that happened when I was a little girl."

"A specific event?"

I nod, my throat tight. "Someone murdered my parents." My voice cracks. "And I was there. But I don't remember it."

Her breathing catches then, just for a second. "And how old were you?"

"Almost three and a half."

Quinn sucks in her lips. She knows who I am, or guesses. But she doesn't ask anything more. "It may be there. It may not be. Memory isn't like a video camera. It doesn't record everything and let you replay it later.

Sometimes if a memory seems to be gone, it really is. Or sometimes it's there, but it's been pushed down, out of conscious thought."

"Do you think you can help me get anything back?"

"I don't know." Lifting her head, she locks eyes with me. "But I can try."

She tells me to sit in one of two facing chairs upholstered in soft apricot. She moves around the room, dimming the lights and closing the blinds. "I'm going to turn on some music." Her voice is low and soothing. "It's not really necessary for the hypnosis, but it gives your ears a neutral background." She presses a button, and instrumental music begins to play.

Then she sits across from me. I realize that all this— the music, the closed blinds, her low and unhurried voice—is the beginning of the process. It's not like in the movies. There's not going to be a watch swinging on a chain. Already I feel different, like I'm separating from myself, observing instead of participating. There's no *I*, no *me*, just *the girl* sinking into the chair. It's like I've gone from first person to third.

In the darkened room, her voice is nearly a whisper. "I'll count to ten. It will be like you're going down a staircase, taking one step with each number. Each step will take you deeper, and when I say ten, you'll be in a place where you're fully relaxed."

"Should I close my eyes?"

"You can keep them open and just focus on my face. Your subconscious will tell you when it's time to close them."

As instructed, I keep my gaze on her while she begins

126

to count to ten. After each number, she says I'm doing great or that the tension is leaving my body. I keep looking at her face. I feel anxious, wondering if I should cheat and just close my eyes. But I keep focused on her. A long stare in a darkened room, but there is no intimacy in it at all. Quinn is only a place to rest my gaze. Slowly her face grows hazy.

When she says, "Five," I blink, and her face changes. Her eyes appear to be covered by a sparkly red mask, but it doesn't seem strange. I blink again, and her face is a man's, complete with a goatee. Another blink, and her features morph into a butterfly.

And then I blink and don't open my eyes again. It takes me a few seconds to realize they're closed.

"Ten," she says. "Good. That's right. You are completely relaxed."

I feel like I do just before I go to sleep, when the horizons of my mind widen.

"Now one of your hands will begin to feel heavy and one light." Both my hands feel heavy and warm upon the arms of the chair. "The hand that feels light might begin to lift itself off the chair, maybe a finger or the whole hand."

I monitor my hands. They're anchored to the chair. I'm failing at this.

"And the arm that is heavy, it's very weighty and stiff, as if it were made of granite. And your arm that is light, it's like a feather—it just wants to float up in the air."

My right hand twitches into life and then rises, higher and higher, until it's over my head. There's no sense of effort, no strain. It doesn't even seem like I'm moving it. The breeze of the air conditioner eddies around it.

I begin to feel as if I am spinning in my chair, even though it doesn't have wheels, even though it's absolutely still. Around and around. It's like being drunk, only I'm not dizzy.

"Now you will have a cheerful, pleasant memory from when you were three," Quinn says. "Of a time when your parents are still alive."

I have a flash: two tiny legs from the knees downward, wearing red socks and blue shoes. Walking. Each of my hands is in a big hand. Two adult voices say in unison, "One, two, three!" The hands lift me up so I swing in midair, held aloft.

I grin.

"That's good, Olivia. And now you will have a memory about the day your parents died."

My eyes dart wildly under closed lids.

"You are safe here, Olivia. You are safe and completely relaxed. Your memories cannot harm you. You're an observer, that's all."

I see more legs. Two sets of adult legs, both in blue jeans, facing each other. I'm standing behind one of the people, and I'm little. White snow all around. The person who is farthest away from me steps closer, so the two sets of knees touch.

"No," a voice says, and I know it's my mom's voice. She says it quietly. Desperately. Earlier there had been yelling. I tilt my head up to see what's happening. My mom steps back from the other person, but then there's a gloved hand on the nape of her neck, pulling her in close. So close. They're dancing. Her arms slice through the air, windmilling as they do when we put on music and dance in the living room.

Something lands on my face. It's like rain, only hot. When I touch it, my fingertips come away red.

At first I think it's paint, but that doesn't make sense. Then I know it's raining blood, pockmarking the snow. The white underneath their boots is turning scarlet.

And my mother is making a noise, but it isn't words. It's beyond words.

I turn and run into the woods.

CHAPTER 26

TRUST YOUR GUT

"TWO! ONE!" QUINN SAYS FROM SOMEWHERE outside where I am. I'm scrambling in the snow, falling, crying, trying to leave the blood behind. "One!" Her voice is urgent, a compressed shout. "You will leave the trance now, Olivia. You're safe."

As if someone has just cut the string, my right hand falls down by my side. Slowly I become aware of where I am. Of *when* I am. I'm panting, breathing as hard as if I really had been running through the woods instead of just remembering.

I open my eyes and straighten up. Try to slow my breathing.

"What did you see?" Quinn leans forward.

"I saw . . ." I have to swallow before I can continue. "Two people in the woods. Standing close together. My mom and someone else. She kept saying no, but the other person pulled her close and stabbed her." I raise my hand to my face, half expecting to still feel the blood freckling my cheeks. "And then I ran." The terror races through me again.

Putting my hands over my face, I try to put in order the memories I've had since I've been back. My mom reading to me. The fresh snow. My mom being stabbed as the churned snow turned red. The bloody knife on the floor mat.

"Did you recognize the other person? Did you see their face?"

Opening my eyes, I shake my head. Quinn's eyes are the color of gas flames. I'm shivering, a tremble so fine it's like I'm vibrating. "Only their legs. I guess because I was little. I couldn't see either of their faces. And I didn't understand what was going on until it was too late. I don't think I really understood until now."

Quinn blows air through pursed lips. "No three-year-old should ever have to understand that." She thinks for a minute. "Even if you didn't see the other person's face, did you hear them speak?"

"No. Like I knew they had been yelling at each other, but in that little bit of memory, the only voice I heard was my mom's. And she just kept saying no." I grab Quinn's hand. Her thin fingers are ice-cold. "Put me back under. If I can go back, I might see the killer's face. I might know who did it."

Sucking in a breath, she pulls her hand back. "I'm so sorry, Olivia, but I have another client coming in ten minutes. Even if I didn't, it's not like there's a dial I can set to take you back to an exact time. Remember, there's no guarantee you even retained the memory of the killer's face or voice. I could take you back over and over, and it might not do anything but cause you a lot of pain."

"But I could still have the memories," I insist, my jaw tight.

"Let me ask you something," Quinn says slowly. "Who else knows?"

"What do you mean?"

"Who else knows what you're trying to find out?"

"Just one person. But he won't say anything. And I guess now you know. Why?"

Her answer is blunt. "Because if whoever did it is still around, they're not going to like you trying to find answers."

"But I'm not the only one who's trying to figure out what happened. At least not since my dad's jawbone was found. The police are reopening the case."

"That's from the outside looking in. You were right there. You were an eyewitness. Even if you didn't retain the memories, if whoever did this finds out about you, they're going to want to stop you. You could be in danger."

"I'm being careful. I have a different name now, first and last, and my hair's a different color. But my parents deserve justice. *I* deserve justice." I square my jaw. "So when can I come back?"

With a sigh, Quinn picks up her appointment calendar. "My next opening's Monday at eleven."

I swear under my breath. "I'm scheduled to work that day."

We go back and forth until we find a time that works for both of us, but it's more than a week away.

"I don't want to wait that long."

"You might not have to." Quinn looks at me appraisingly.

"What do you mean?"

"After a session, many people have revelations, both in dreams and while awake. Some obvious and some not so obvious. Write them down. Keep track of them." She leans closer. "Trust your gut."

CHAPTER 27

A STORY GOING AROUND

I HAVE TO GO TO WORK, BUT ONCE I'M AT Fred Meyer, I move like an automaton. Duncan texts me from Zumiez, wanting to know what I learned, but I respond that it's too long to explain in a text. I'm working in the prep room when my coworker Andy snaps his fingers and says my name.

"Huh?" I follow his pointing finger. I've just tossed a trimmed bunch of celery into the garbage while keeping the pared-off brown and broken bits on the cutting board. "Oops!" I retrieve the bunch and rinse it off.

"Are you okay?" he asks. Andy has worked here forever, and he's always warning me to lift with my legs and be careful with the produce knives.

"Just didn't sleep well, that's all." In my head, I'm still watching my mother flail her arms while her blood rains onto the snow.

"I hear you. It's been so hot." He takes a paper towel and runs it over his red face and what remains of his hair. "Even the air-conditioning here isn't keeping up."

I don't feel it. I'm stuck in the bone-chilling cold of my memories.

A half hour later, Duncan comes in, his face full of curiosity. I ask Andy if it's okay for me to go on break, then take off my apron and ball it up. "Come on, let's get out of here."

I don't speak until we're alone in the cookware aisle. "The hypnotist was able to take me back to that day, but I guess nothing about it is exact. Not what ends up in your memory, not where she can get you to go. But"—I have to swallow before I can continue—"I saw it happen. I saw my mom's murder. And now I know why I told my grandma that she was dancing."

"Why?" Duncan breathes.

"Because she was pinwheeling her arms, trying to get away, but the killer was yanking her close." I demonstrate, feeling her helplessness in my own body.

"Oh my God." Duncan grabs my wrist, his eyes widening. "So you saw the killer?"

Still feeling the echoes of my mom, I step back and pull my arm away. "I was only three, remember? Probably no taller than this." I put my hand at hip level. "They were both wearing jeans and boots. And that's all I saw: their legs, and my mom's back and arms, and her blood falling onto the snow. And then I guess I started freaking out, both in the past and now, because the hypnotist woke me up."

"Do you think it was someone you knew? Was it a man or a woman? Was your dad there?"

"I don't know," I say miserably. "I don't know, I don't know, I don't know. I was trying to run away. But I guess the killer must have caught me." I shiver, remembering the bloody knife on the floor of a car.

"That must have been awful, having to relive that." He pulls me into a hug, and this time I don't pull away. My shoulders tremble against his chest.

A second later, a surprised voice says, "Duncan?" We step apart. It's a woman with a thick brown braid almost to her waist. She's wearing a green apron that matches the one I'm holding.

Color rises in Duncan's cheeks. "Oh, hi, Mom. Um, Mom, this is Olivia. She's Nora's new neighbor."

I almost put out my hand, then remember the scar and think better of it. I just say, "Nice to meet you, Mrs.—"

"Call me Audrey." Her eyes are still going back and forth between Duncan and me. It's clear she's imagining much more between us than there really is. "So you're Nora's neighbor, huh? If you've just moved into the neighborhood, then you might not know about the big barbecue we have every summer. It's this Friday at six. I don't know if Duncan's invited you yet, but you should come."

"Thank you." I try to sound perky and normal, like I wasn't just talking about blood raining on the snow. "That sounds fun. I can come over after I get off at eight. Should I bring something?"

"Don't worry about it." She waves a slender hand. "Just bring yourself."

"We'd better get going, Mom," Duncan says. "Olivia's on break, and she wanted to go to Starbucks."

We say good-bye. Once we're out of his mom's

earshot, I say, "I get the feeling your mom wants a chance to check me out."

Duncan's cheeks get even redder. "I've been thinking: If we pretended to be boyfriend and girlfriend, it could be a good cover for us spending time together."

"Maybe," I say, drawing the word out. Before the cops showed up at my door, I would have wanted to be far more than Duncan's pretend girlfriend. But now finding my parents' killer is the only thing that matters.

"And the party will give *you* a chance to check out people. Half of Medford comes. Even Chief Spaulding. Everybody's going to be talking about the murders."

At Starbucks, I order a grande latte, hoping it will warm me up. I also get a scone, since I got up too late to have breakfast. We sit in an empty corner.

Duncan takes a sip of his iced coffee. "I was talking about it with my dad this morning. He said there's a story going around about Samantha."

"Sam?"

"I guess when she was in high school, her mom had to work two jobs because her dad was basically a drunk. Once Sam and her dad got in this big fight. After they saw blood on her sweater, the neighbors thought he had hurt her and called the police. Only it turned out that she was the one who'd hurt him." Duncan sucks in a breath. "And get this—she *stabbed* him."

"What?"

"Dad said it was just a paring knife, and her dad refused to press charges. Still, my dad said people are talking about it now."

Even Duncan must be starting to realize that just because you know someone doesn't mean they can't be a killer. "So Sam and Jason," I ask. "Do they come to this party your parents throw?"

"Every year."

CHAPTER 28

A LOT OF CASH

WHEN I CLOCK OUT, I'M STARVING. ALL I'VE had to eat today is that scone at Starbucks, as well as some unsalable produce, which I ate over the prep sink. Half an apple with a wormhole in the other half. A chunk of watermelon too mangled to wrap in plastic. A carrot that looked like two legs and a torso. All the imperfect things no one wants to buy, as if everything has to be free of bruises and blemishes or it's worthless.

There's a McDonald's just down the street. When I walk in, my mom's old best friend, Heather, is sitting at a table for four. Her eyes slide over me, like she's waiting for someone and I'm nothing but a vague disappointment. With a sigh, she looks back down at her phone and picks up a limp french fry from one of two half-eaten Happy Meals on the other side of the table.

After I get my order, I take the next table over so that I'm sitting with my back to her. I get out my phone and pretend to be engrossed in it, tilting my head to let my hair obscure my face.

Jason hurries in. Heather's ex-husband. My dad's best friend. My mom's old crush? And just maybe a serial killer.

"You're late," Heather says in a flat voice.

"You can't blame it on me, Heather. For once." Jason slides into a seat across from her so that we're sitting back-to-back. "I would have been here on time except I had to swing the rig wide to make a right turn, and then some idiot tried to pass me on the left. I had to cut back over so I wouldn't hit her, and then I couldn't make the turn. It took me forever to get through. No one would move."

"And that made you nearly an hour late?" She bites off each word.

"Don't you get on my case, too. The company already did. All they care about is moving freight. They're always watching me. I know the dispatcher talks about me behind my back. Between how little they pay me and how much I have to give you, I'm basically a homeless guy living in a truck." He pauses. "Where are the kids, anyway?"

"In the play structure. They got bored waiting for you."

Through our connected seats, I can feel him continually shifting. "Have the cops talked to you yet?"

"I talked to Stephen two days ago, but I didn't have anything new to tell him."

Jason lowers his voice. "Did he ask about me?"

"He asked about everyone. But who can remember exactly what everyone was doing fourteen years ago?"

"So you didn't tell him anything?"

"No, Jason!" Heather's tone changes, becomes more uncertain. "What is there to tell?"

"Nothing. Forget I said anything." He grunts. "About the only thing we know for sure is it wasn't Terry. It could have been any of us, couldn't it?"

"What do you mean?"

"Terry and Naomi might have taken someone with them. Some friend of theirs. Which means it would be a friend of ours."

"Jason." She heaves an exasperated sigh. "Can you stop being so paranoid? It wasn't one of us. Naomi and Terry—they must have just run into some bad guy. Some crazy psycho killer out in the woods."

"Why would a stranger kill them?" Jason asks.

"Why does a psycho kill anyone? Because that's what they do. All I know is that no one I know would be capable of doing"—she hesitates—"that."

"What about Rich?"

Heather lets out a surprised bark of laughter. "What would Richard have to do with it?"

"Right after Terry and Naomi went missing, I noticed Rich's knuckles were bruised. Like he'd been fighting. And remember how he always used to wear thrift store clothes and scrounge for meals? Now he's just like his name—rich. Everything started to change for him around the time Terry and Naomi died. You have to ask yourself why."

"But that doesn't make any sense. Those two didn't have any money."

"That's not true," Jason retorts. "I've been thinking back about what was happening then. Terry had been pulling a lot of double shifts so he could catch up on child support. I wouldn't be surprised if he was carrying a couple of thousand that day."

Is Jason right? Could money have been a motive after all? Or is Jason just trying to make sure no one looks too closely at him?

CHAPTER 29

DISCARDED

THE NEXT MORNING, DUNCAN TEXTS ME before work. "Look at the *Mail Tribune*. Evidence got ruined."

With a sinking feeling, I turn on my laptop.

**WITH EVIDENCE DISCARDED,
NEW LEADS SOUGHT IN DEATHS OF TWO**

Nearly fourteen years after the deaths of twenty-year-old Naomi Benson and twenty-one-year-old Terry Weeks in the Cascade Range, friends and family are hoping that the recent discovery of some of Weeks's remains will help jump-start the cold case. Weeks had long been suspected in Benson's murder, but now authorities believe both were killed by the same person.

Medford's chief of police is asking for help in finding their killer. "No matter how small or insignificant it may seem to somebody, it could be an important lead," says Chief Stephen Spaulding. He says he wants to know of any individuals who changed their patterns since the murders—maybe moved, quit their jobs, or stopped visiting the forest where the bodies were found.

Although advances have been made in retrieving even minute amounts of DNA in cold cases, Spaulding said that won't be possible here. "A few years ago we had a pipe break in the evidence room, and it left some case files completely waterlogged. Unfortunately, this was one of those cases. All the fabric items associated with those cases— including Naomi's clothing and the tarp she was found in—became severely contaminated with mold and had to be discarded."

So that's it, then. No fibers. No fingerprints. No DNA.

But I think about what Jason said, what the police chief asked. I wonder if anyone has pointed out to him just how much Richard's life has changed since my parents' murders.

CHAPTER 30

ARE THEY REALLY THAT DIFFERENT?

A COUPLE OF DAYS LATER, I'M WALKING into work when I spot Sam in the parking lot. The girl who stabbed her own father. The woman who is now even higher on my list of suspects.

She's loading a bag of groceries and a case of Coke Zero into the trunk of her car. It's a silver Audi, as sleek and understated as she is. She's wearing high-heeled sandals and a short-sleeved black dress that skims her thin figure. Would those slender arms be capable of plunging a knife into my mother so many times? Fighting her drunk dad would be one thing. Killing two people while their kid watched would be something else entirely.

She returns the cart to the corral, then leans against the metal railing, rummages in her purse, and comes up with a red-and-white pack of cigarettes. Unfiltered Marlboros. She taps one out, lights it, and draws the smoke in so hard her thin face becomes just plain gaunt.

This is my chance to talk with her, to see if I can shake

loose the truth. With my apron tucked under my arm, I walk over to her before I can change my mind. "Mind if I bum a cigarette before I have to go to work?"

Her laugh has a lot of gravel in it. "You're too young to be smoking."

"I'm eighteen," I lie.

"Uh-huh." She looks me up and down. "Eighteen's still too young. If everyone waited until they were twenty-one before they picked up a cigarette, no one would ever be a smoker. They hook you while you're young and stupid and you think you'll live forever. Trust me, I know."

Despite her words, Sam hands me a cigarette and her lighter. It's heavy and silver. I manage to light up without too much fumbling. I used to smoke a little back in middle school, back when I wanted to fit in with a certain crowd, even if it was the kind of crowd most kids didn't want to join. The yeah-I-smoke, yeah-I-pierced-my-own-ears/nose/lip, yeah-my-friend-made-this-tattoo crowd.

Eventually I realized it was all a little stupid, and I stopped. I still have what's supposed to be a ghost-bat on my biceps, although it actually doesn't look much like either.

She sucks down another lungful and then sticks out her hand. "I'm Sam."

"Olivia." We shake hands lightly. I'm mostly pretending to smoke, not wanting to start coughing.

"You were at Terry's funeral." She looks at me more closely, and I try to maintain a neutral expression. Do

146

those cool blue eyes belong to a killer? "So do I know your parents or something?"

I shake my head. "I just moved into Naomi Benson's old house. The neighbor, Nora Murdoch, wasn't feeling well that day. She asked me to drive her."

"Naomi wasn't much older than you when she was murdered. She had these high cheekbones." Sam touches her own face as she keeps looking at me. "Kind of like yours."

Just as I'm starting to panic, the answer comes to me like a gift. "Was she part Native American? Because I am." I have no idea if that's true. I change the subject both to distract Sam and to ask what I really want to know. "So who do you think killed them? I've heard all kinds of theories since I moved in. I've started reading up on the case, trying to figure out what happened."

She blows a stream of smoke sideways. This close, I can see how carefully her face is made up, every square centimeter covered with a thin layer of foundation or eye shadow or blush.

"I wasn't that close to them, at least not Naomi. Terry and I used to hang around together when we were younger, but I hadn't talked to him in the months before it happened."

Is she lying, or was the person I overheard at the funeral? Or is it all just a matter of how you see things, what you choose to remember?

"Didn't you say something at the service about spending time with him at the river?"

"Yeah. In high school. But then I went to community

147

college and got a job selling real estate, and Terry started working at the mill. Things change when you get older. You grow up. You grow apart."

"Still, you must have some guesses about what happened to them." I keep my eyes on the glowing ash of my cigarette, not wanting to look too eager.

Sam pauses for a moment, then says, "I kind of wonder if they should be looking at Jason."

A thrill goes through me, but I squint as though I'm trying to remember. "Wasn't that the guy who was Terry's best friend?"

"Yeah. He was also more than a little in love with Naomi. Not to speak ill of the dead, but I don't know what everyone saw in her." Sam's mouth twists. I saw her picture in the annual. Sam was just as striking back then, and far less brittle than she is now. Sure, my mom was pretty, but she also looked young and unfinished. Even when Sam was seventeen, she already looked like an adult, cool and self-contained. Her voice interrupts my thoughts. "Jason used to carry a knife everywhere."

And he's a trucker. Still, Duncan had a point when he argued against this idea. "But why would Jason do it? Kill his best friend?"

"Maybe they had some kind of fight over her. Maybe he killed Terry, and then he had to kill Naomi."

"If he was in love with Naomi, why would he stab her so many times?"

"All it takes is once." She exhales twin streams of smoke.

"What?" I'm not following, at least not consciously, but the back of my neck prickles.

"If you stabbed somebody once, it would already be too late. You couldn't stop. You would just have to keep stabbing until it was done. Even if it took nineteen times." Sam turns her icy blue eyes to me as she stubs out her cigarette on the metal rail. "Love, hate—are they really that different?"

CHAPTER 31

WICKED-LOOKING THORNS

WHEN I ANSWER THE KNOCK ON MY DOOR the next day, Nora's standing on the front porch. The doubling thing happens again as I remember opening the door to find the old Nora, wanting to visit with my grandmother.

"Want to go for a walk in the cemetery?" she asks.

"Sure. I don't have to be at work for nearly two hours." Anything that will get me outside my own head sounds good. My dreams last night were an endless loop of my mom trying to escape her killer. Quinn said I would have new revelations, but I seem stuck on the old.

Despite her long legs, Nora takes tiny steps as we go down the hill and then turn onto the flat dirt road that leads to the cemetery. I make a conscious effort to slow my steps.

"I love this old cemetery." She has to pause for breath after each word or two. "It's my favorite place in the world."

I hold the gate for her. To the left, a carefully tended

bed of flowers catches my eye. I walk over to admire it. When I turn back, Nora is still well behind me.

"Are you all right?"

"I might just . . ."—a pause while she gathers another breath—"need to sit down." She collapses more than sits on a low stone wall. I reach out to grab her in case she keeps toppling sideways. She lists but doesn't fall.

Her breathing is too fast and too shallow. Her skin looks so white. Should I run back and get my car so I can drive her home? But what if something happens in the meantime? "Are you okay?"

"I just need to . . ."—another long pause—"rest."

I pretend not to be watching her. The wall we're sitting on surrounds a small family plot that holds three gravestones and has an empty space where a fourth grave could go. The most recent date on any of the tombstones is 1938.

"If I pass out, you have to promise," she says between breaths, "to let me go. Make sure it's a good long time before you call anyone."

Shocked, I lean away from her. "You don't mean that!"

"I'm ready. I've had two heart attacks. My hearing is totally shot. My cataracts are getting worse." She pauses between sentences. "It's like having a car that's starting to nickel-and-dime you. At some point, it's not worth keeping anymore. Besides, I want to see what happens next."

"So you believe in heaven and harps and all that?"

"I don't know if God exists. None of us can really *know*. But I believe he does."

I nod. I'm not so sure about God, but I do believe in

evil. But maybe if you believe in evil, you have to believe in its opposite.

Nora echoes my thoughts. "About the only thing I know is that it all comes down to love. Love is the only thing that matters. It's all there is. But that's plenty." Her voice has strengthened, even if she's still as blue-white as skim milk.

I'm not certain what I believe in. Except maybe Nora.

A woman walking a small dog crests the hill and comes toward us. She's wearing a navy-blue business suit and tennis shoes.

"I don't know her," Nora says, almost to herself. She straightens up as the woman gets closer, then calls, "Hello!"

I smile awkwardly.

The woman stops, but the dog makes a beeline toward Nora. It looks like a collie, black and brown and white, only smaller. It crouches until its belly touches the ground, and then it begins crawling toward Nora, wiggling and squirming to stay flat.

The woman's eyes go wide. "I've never seen her do that before."

Meanwhile, the dog has reached Nora. Now it rolls over on its back, presenting its belly.

"Who's a good dog?" Nora reaches out to scratch the pink skin that shows through the fine white hairs. The dog lets out a cross between a groan and a whine.

"Wow, I would have said she would never let anyone do that." The dog's owner watches as Nora ruffles her fingers back and forth. "Not even me. She would take my hand off for sure."

Nora doesn't answer. She's got eyes and ears only for the dog.

Finally, the woman says, "Bella, we have to go, or I'll be late for work. Come on, Bella." She tugs the leash, and the dog, with one last reluctant whine, gets to its feet. As the lady is walking away, she calls, "You and your granddaughter have a great day."

"We will," Nora says. I manage a nod. Tears prick my eyes. I only wish she were my grandmother. Suddenly, I miss my real grandmother fiercely.

"Do you want to keep going?" Nora gets to her feet. She seems energized by the conversation with the woman and, more important, the woman's dog.

"Sure."

We start off again, Nora's steps still more shuffle than stride. I keep one hand out, ready to grab her elbow. As we start up the low hill, I see a red splotch on my mother's grave. A jolt of excitement races from my head to my heels. I jog toward it for a closer look. It's a single red rose, the color of old blood. It looks fresh. Its stem sports wicked-looking thorns at least a half inch long. I don't think it was bought at a florist's or filched from an arrangement. The end is ragged, not snipped. The rose must have come from a garden.

I bring it back to Nora. "Frank told me he keeps finding red roses on Naomi's grave. This must be one of them."

"Maybe it's from one of your mother's old admirers," Nora says.

I go still inside. "What did you say?"

Nora looks at me for a long time. Finally, I'm the one who has to look away.

She touches my shoulder. "Oh, honey, I've known for a while now."

"Did you see me take that Halloween photo of me and my parents?" I still can't look at her.

Her tone is colored with warmth. "I saw you." I turn to look into her kind face. "Really saw you. Anyone with eyes in their head would see you were Terry and Naomi's daughter. I should have spotted it the first day, no matter what you said your name was."

"My name really is Olivia now." Even though I've lied to everyone, it stings a little that she thinks I lied to her. "The lady who adopted me changed my name."

"Does she know you're here?"

I'm not sure Tamsin even knows I'm alive. "The adoption didn't last. I'm sorry I didn't tell you before. But I want to find out the truth about who killed my parents. I'm starting to figure things out, but people will stop talking if they know who I am." I take a deep breath. "What was she like? Naomi, I mean?"

"She was a smart girl. Kind. A good mother. She read to you, and she loved to make you laugh. Your parents always loved you, even if they didn't always love each other. And I think they did love each other. They were just young."

"I never even got to know her. To know them. Talk to them." My throat closes with tears. "Why didn't the killer take me, too? They might as well have." The shell I've built up in layers around myself over the years has developed too many cracks.

"But you're still standing." She takes my warm hand in her cold one.

We start down the hill. Two men are at the bottom. One is riding a kid's bike that's way too small for him. The other blows his nose into the dirt, which is beyond disgusting, then wipes it on the sleeve of his heavy coat. They both look homeless.

My shoulders hunch. Nora, tottering along in her knockoff Keds, looks like the perfect victim. Neither of us is carrying a purse, but that probably won't stop them. I'm sure they'll ask for money. Or demand it.

We haven't seen anyone else since the woman with her dog. I scan the rest of the cemetery, but it's empty. Even if I were to shout for help, the houses are too far away. I have to be ready to protect Nora. To put myself between them and her.

Nora's been watching her feet, but now she lifts her head, just as the two men notice us.

This is it. I exhale and tense my muscles.

"Benjy!" Nora shouts, waving.

"Flora Nora!" The guy in the heavy coat lopes up to us and gives her a hug. He's got a ruddy face and red hair. I recognize him from the funeral.

"Who's your friend?" she asks him, but the other guy is already riding away from us. And Benjy doesn't answer.

"Benjy, this is Olivia," Nora says, undeterred. "She just moved in next door. Olivia, this is my friend Benjy." The two of them—the age-spotted old woman and the man whose slack mouth has more holes than teeth—don't belong together. At least not in my head. But in hers, it's clear they do.

She still has her arm around his waist, but he's not looking at me. Instead, he's staring at the rose in my hand.

155

This close, his sunburned face is familiar. I flash back on the red-haired guy in the yearbook photo of my parents and their friends. Now I see the resemblance between this dirty, homeless man and that boy.

"You're Ben Gault, aren't you?" I ask.

He doesn't answer, but his eyes go wide. Pulling free from Nora, he turns and begins to run away.

CHAPTER 32

A BROKEN STAGGER

"BEN!" I SHOUT. "HEY, WAIT A MINUTE! BENJY! Can I please just talk to you?"

He keeps running. "I'll be right back," I tell Nora, and then sprint after him. In his heavy coat and falling-apart shoes, he's not very fast.

Finally, he stops and turns toward me with his hands up. He's trembling. "I'm not hurting anything."

"It's okay. Don't be frightened. It's just that I saw you at Terry Weeks's funeral, and I want to ask you a couple of questions. You're Ben Gault, right?"

He shakes his head. "The guy whose name's on my birth certificate is dead."

I blink. "But you *are* Ben Gault, right? You were friends with Terry Weeks and Naomi Benson?"

"Ben Gault, that's just a noise." His hands fall loose by his sides. "A sound. It doesn't mean anything. Of course, the government comes looking for Ben every now and then, but that's okay. I no longer have anything to hide. I don't steal. I don't even beg. I feel the eyes on me, though."

He makes a V with two fingers, points it at me, and then turns to tap it on his forehead. "I hear people talking about me." The whites of his eyes are the only clean-looking part of his face. "That's why I have the earplugs. So I can sleep at night. But the voices sneak in anyway."

He's clearly off. Mentally ill? Asperger's? On drugs? But he doesn't seem dangerous, and Nora considers him a friend. And he might know something about my mom. "Can I just ask you something? About Naomi?"

His eyes narrow. "Don't look at me with those please-help-me eyes. Out here, you can't be all nicey-nicey."

I hold out the rose. "Did you leave this at Naomi's grave?"

"I didn't steal it."

"I believe you. But why did you leave it?"

"She listens to me."

The present tense makes me shiver. I repeat what Frank told me. "I heard that you talk to her gravestone."

"I don't talk to her gravestone." His laugh is gently mocking. "I talk to Naomi. You think the dead don't hear? You think they don't talk back? Nora knows what I'm talking about."

A sudden odd hope fills me. What if he's right? When I leaned down to pick up the rose, if I had listened hard enough, would I have heard my mom's voice? What would she have said?

"What does she tell you?" I ask, but Benjy just looks at me blankly. "What does Naomi say to you?"

The light is gone from his eyes now. "The dead leave you alone, unknown, bones, no phones, rolling stones. Only there *is* moss."

His words make a kind of strange sense, even down to the moss. Many of the words chiseled on the old headstones have been filled in by lichen. "So Naomi doesn't say anything to you?"

"She knows I'll be there soon."

I flinch. "Don't say that. You're still young." He doesn't look young, though. The dirt ground into his face emphasizes the lines on his forehead, around his eyes, bracketing his mouth. Maybe street years are like dog years.

A puzzled look comes over his face, and he takes a step closer. Involuntarily, I step back, but then he takes two, until he's nearly close enough to kiss me. He smells like sweat and pee and mothballs, like something forgotten, rotting in a greenhouse.

"Naomi?" He tilts his head so far to the side it looks like it will come off his neck.

He's not asking a question about her. He's asking a question *of* me.

He thinks I'm my mom.

"No, my name's Olivia. Naomi's dead."

"Naomi!" He grabs my hand so hard the bones grind together. It's all I can do not to pull away. "I'm sorry," he says. "I'm sorry, I'm sorry, I'm sorry."

I force out the words. "What are you sorry for, Benjy?"

"You know." He looks away, breaking eye contact. His mouth curls down at the corners as if he's going to cry.

"I don't. Tell me. Tell me what happened to Naomi. Tell me." I have to swallow before I can go on. "Tell me what happened to me."

"After, I looked for you."

I interpret. "You were one of the people who looked

159

for evidence. After"—I can't bring myself to say *my*—"the body was found."

"We were out in the woods, the woods, the trees were watching, so I watched, too. And I saw—I saw."

"What did you see?" Which *we* is he talking about? Is he saying he was with my parents when it happened? Or does he mean the search?

He looks past me with unfocused eyes. "In the daytime, when I go outside, I used to show my friends what they hadn't seen before. Like the hello, see you later, like the halo, when I was twenty, when I began preaching the truth." With his free hand, he points above my head. "See, the light which is your halo." He leans closer, and his sour breath washes over me. "You know, aura. That's why everyone can't see that. If you, if you got some of the drugs, maybe you can see, maybe you can't." His face twists with anguish. "I know what I saw. Everyone knows what they see. But I don't know what's for real or not."

"What did you see, Benjy?" My blood chills. "What did you see?"

"Orange trucks suffer. Snow blood dogs hand in glove"—he looks up from our linked hands to me—"run. They say run!" He lets go, turns, and begins to run again, a broken stagger.

I watch him go, feeling as if I've been underwater, drowning, and now I've come back up for air. Come back to reality.

I realize I should never have left Nora alone. What if she's fallen while I've been gone? Had a heart attack?

What if the other homeless guy has come back for her? I break into a run.

I find her sitting on a bench. It's a relief to see that her color is better.

"Sorry I left you."

"You took off like your hair was on fire. How do you know Benjy? What did you want to ask him?"

"He was friends with my parents, and Frank says he talks to my mom's tombstone. I tried to ask him about it, but he didn't make much sense. About all I understood was that maybe he saw something in the woods back then. Or thinks he did."

"He may not know, himself," Nora says. "He's gone in and out of reality for years. At least the reality we understand. To him, it's always real."

Where does the truth lie? Is Benjy terrified by what he saw? By what he imagines he saw?

Or could it even be by what he did?

CHAPTER 33

THE GIRL I USED TO BE

THE DAY IS JUST BEGINNING TO COOL OFF as I head home to get ready for the party at Duncan's house. After a quick shower, I dress in cutoffs and the white peasant blouse I got at Goodwill and put on Nora's necklace again. I've been wearing it every day. She told me earlier that she doesn't have the energy to go to the barbecue tonight.

Since it's only six blocks away, I decide to walk, and I text Duncan that I'm on my way. Carrying a bowl of grapes, I set off down the hill, past the old cemetery. Soon the mouthwatering smell of grilled meat fills the air. The street is full of cars, and the yard is full of people.

Duncan steps out on the porch. When he sees me, his face lights up and he waves. I remind myself that we are only pretending to be boyfriend and girlfriend. I weave around clumps of people, recognizing some faces from the memorial. Stephen Spaulding, the police chief, is deep in conversation with Sam. His black pants and polo shirt still look like a uniform.

The house is lived in and comfortable, with hardwood floors, a well-used leather couch, and books everywhere. In the kitchen, Duncan's mom is digging in the fridge but straightens up when she sees us. She's dressed in jeans and a sleeveless top. Her feet are bare.

"Nice to see you again, Olivia." I feel her eyes measuring me before she turns to her son. "Hey, Duncan, I was sure we had a new bottle of ketchup. Have you seen it?"

He shakes his head.

I hold out the bowl of grapes. "Where should I put these? They're already washed."

"That was sweet of you! The food goes in the backyard, which is where all the kids are hanging out." She turns to Duncan. "Although I guess you guys are a little too old to run through the sprinkler or toss the beanbag."

"You're never too old to cornhole," says a man holding a spatula as he comes in through the sliding glass door. His dark hair is cut close to his scalp, and his eyes are such a pale gray they're almost silver. I only need to look from him to Duncan to know it's his dad.

He sticks out his hand, which is covered with dozens of tiny cuts in various stages of healing. "Hi. I'm Gregg. With three Gs. Which can be confusing to some people."

I hold up my bowl of grapes as an excuse not to shake hands. I need to be careful that neither of his parents notices my scar. "Hi, Gregg with three Gs. I'm Olivia with a bunch of vowels."

He grins. "Good thing neither of us is a Scrabble word."

"Olivia just moved into the house Terry's wife used to live in," Duncan says.

"You mean Terry's girlfriend? Naomi Benson?" he asks. "Naomi and Terry were never married."

"Yeah, Naomi's house," I say. "Hers and her mother's." I don't mention me. "Did you know them well?"

Gregg takes a second spatula from a crock on the counter. "Audrey knew Naomi better than I did. Terry used to live next door with his dad, so the three of us went hunting together a few times." He hands the spatula to Duncan. "Can you come help me out at the grill? Everyone's ready for round two."

As they leave, Audrey says, "Naomi and Terry's little girl used to play with Duncan."

I want to keep the focus on my parents, not on the girl I used to be. I steer the conversation back around. "What was Naomi like?"

"She was pretty. Quiet. Smart." As she speaks, she opens the refrigerator again and leans in, shuffling containers and bottles. "When she got pregnant, she started knitting all these little booties and sweaters." Her voice is muffled. "Terry was more a life-of-the-party type guy. When they said he killed her, we didn't want to believe it, but then again, you never want to believe stuff like that."

"The paper said the police had been called out to the house several times and that she actually had a restraining order against him."

Audrey looks over her shoulder at me. "That was Naomi's mom, Sharon. She was mad at Terry for getting Naomi pregnant, and then he got behind on child support. That Thanksgiving, everyone had too much to drink and there was a shoving match. Sharon called the cops and insisted Naomi press charges. Terry told us about it. He was embarrassed and ashamed."

I feel a surge of hope, even if it's based on the idea of my parents having a drunken argument and my grandmother lying. "So they didn't really fight?"

"Ah! There it is! I knew I had another one!" Triumphantly brandishing a bottle of ketchup, Audrey emerges from the fridge. She turns to me. "Oh, yeah, they fought. Gregg and I fought all the time back then, too, and we were a few years older. Naomi and Terry were still kids themselves when their baby was born. Gregg and me—we got a chance to grow up. To figure things out. They didn't." With the ketchup bottle, she points at the sliding glass door. "Come on, let's go outside and get you some food."

Taking the grapes, I follow her. On one side of the crowded backyard, squealing kids run through a sprinkler. The water sparkles in the long rays of the setting sun. On the other, people are pulling drinks from an ice-filled cooler or circling a picnic table still crowded with food.

Chicken breasts and hamburger patties sizzle as Duncan and his dad turn them on a huge stainless-steel grill. Hovering over the meat is Richard Lee, dressed in crisp blue Bermudas and a madras plaid short-sleeved shirt. When he catches sight of me, he gives me something between a wave and a salute. He looks so different from the ragged boy in the annual. Had his change in circumstances really started with my parents' murder?

I move a nearly empty bag of Doritos to make room

for my grapes. Sam is in the backyard now, adding a scoop of potato salad to an already-heaping plate. Where is she going to put it? You could cut yourself on her shinbones.

From across the yard, Lauren gives me a little wave, and I walk over to her, relieved to talk to one person who for sure can't be a suspect.

"You're wearing that blouse! And your necklace is beautiful." She squints. "Are those buttons?"

"Thanks. They are." I run my fingers over them. "Nora gave it to me." Lauren's wearing shorts and a yellow T-shirt that would look terrible on me. On her, it just sets off her tanned skin and purple hair.

She scans the crowd. "Is she here? I haven't seen her yet."

"No. She decided not to come. She said she didn't want to be out too late."

"Too late? It's not even nine o'clock."

"I think that's about when she goes to bed. But she gets up before dawn." My stomach rumbles. "I'm going to get something to eat. I didn't have much lunch today."

As I circle the table, I try to eavesdrop. I'm pretty sure I catch my parents' names a few times, but whenever I get closer, people fall silent.

Jason is saying to Carly, "When you're out on the open road, and it's just you and your big, powerful truck, the feeling is amazing." He labors over his pronunciation, his features bunched together. The beer he's holding clearly isn't his first. "Basically, I'm getting paid to cruise along while jamming to my favorite tunes." I remember him complaining about his job to Heather. Maybe he's good at presenting only the side he wants people to see.

But Carly's not really listening. Instead, she says, "Terry would have loved this party, wouldn't he?"

At the sound of my father's name, Sam lifts her head from her plate. "He would probably be leading us all in a conga line or something." Her smile is lopsided.

Jason swears. "Nothing's been the same since he died."

Is Sam's or Jason's grief a cover for something darker? And what about Richard? Did his real estate empire start with my father's money? And did Benjy really see anything in the woods—or is he the victim of his own mind? Despite what Quinn said about revelations, I feel that I'm no closer to the truth than when I started.

CHAPTER 34

THINGS HAVE CHANGED

S AM IMMEDIATELY FORKS A BRATWURST onto her plate when Duncan sets a platter piled high with meat on the table. He comes over to me and leans in.

"Learning anything?"

"I've been trying to eavesdrop, but people are too good about keeping their conversations private."

"I've got an idea." He tugs my wrist. "Come with me."

I follow him around the corner until we're at the base of an oak tree that starts in the side yard and hangs over the backyard. About eight feet up, it forks into two massive trunks. A thin knotted rope dangles down the center, where three warped boards are nailed like a ladder. Bridging the gap between the two trunks is a weathered tree house, maybe six feet long and not quite as tall, with a big open window and a peaked roof.

"When you're up there, you can see and hear everything," he says, "but nobody notices you."

I run my thumb over my scar. "Is this the tree I was climbing when I fell?"

"Yeah. Me and my dad built the tree house the next year."

Grabbing the rope, I give it an experimental tug. It holds firm. A few seconds later, I pull myself up onto the open platform that serves as the tree house's front porch. On hands and knees, I crawl inside. There's an old pink quilt, a wooden folding chair, a brown cushion, and two unlit votive candles.

I'm still taking it all in when Duncan scrambles in behind me.

I turn my head to ask him something. He's a lot closer than I thought, and my nose grazes his cheek. Suddenly, we're kissing. I think it surprises him as much as it surprises me.

My whole body starts to hum. I no longer hear the sounds of the party below us, no longer feel the rough boards under my hands and bare knees. When Duncan lifts his lips from mine, it's like waking from a dream.

When I open my eyes, he's blinking. "Wow!" he says softly, sitting back on his heels and running his thumb over his lips.

When I start to sway, he grabs my arm above the elbow. Then he freezes. It's not something he sees. It's something he hears.

"I can't believe it's been fourteen years," Carly is saying. "Fourteen years. I've missed my brother every single day."

"There was no one like him," Richard says.

"Every time I got an e-mail message from an address I didn't know or a call from a number I didn't recognize, I thought it might be him." Carly's voice trembles.

Someone makes a strangled sound. I think it might be Sam.

"A lot of things have changed in the last fourteen years," Jason says. There's an edge to his tone. "And a lot of people."

Duncan and I lean forward until we can see below. No one looks up. They're too focused on one another.

"What do you mean?" Audrey asks.

Jason points an accusing finger at Richard. "Back in the day, you were as raggedy-ass as the rest of us. You used to hang around my house at dinnertime, hoping to be invited to eat. Now you're *Richard*"—he gives the full name a sarcastic spin—"and you've got your face on billboards, and every time I turn on the TV, there's your commercial. Look at you, with your plaid shirt and fancy watch. The rest of us are still scraping along, and you look like an actor."

Richard lifts his chin. "I worked hard to get where I am."

"So are you saying we don't?" Jason waves one hand at the rest of the group. "Everyone else is working their butts off and has been forever, but right after Naomi and Terry died, things started to change for you. Terry'd been pulling double shifts so he could pay off his back child support. He told me he was going to give the money to Naomi before Christmas. You think no one remembers how your hands were all banged up that Monday after they disappeared? Like you'd been fighting. I think you stole that money—and then you killed them!"

Duncan and I exchange a wide-eyed look.

"Please, Jason." Sam pushes herself to her feet. Her voice is as sharp as a razor. "Richard may be a money-grubber, but he'd never get his hands dirty like that. He's got a little system going. He finds some old lady who's behind on her property taxes, who's maybe not thinking so clearly. Then he makes her a deal: He pays the taxes, and she signs the house over to him. When she dies, he sells the house and keeps the profit, and the heirs get nothing." She shakes her head in disgust. "And he'll tell you that it's all perfectly legal."

I remember seeing Frank shake his finger at Richard after the memorial.

Richard draws himself up to his full height and smooths the front of his shirt. "How I got where I am is all legal. And some of those people have gotten far more out of me than I get in return." His face contorts into a sneer. "As for my knuckles, Jason, they were bruised because I finally stopped letting my mom's boyfriend beat me. I was nowhere near the woods that day, and I have no idea what happened to Terry and Naomi. But I never believed Terry did it. Can the rest of you say the same?" He stares at the ring of faces and then stalks off.

CHAPTER 35

LOST CAUSE

I TURN AROUND TO SEE WHAT DUNCAN thinks. At first he looks shocked, but when his gaze shifts to me, his features soften. He's clearly remembering the kiss we just shared. I need someone who can help me—not kiss me. "I have to go." My words sound abrupt, even to my own ears.

I climb down the tree and go inside the house, mentally berating myself. I'm not here to make out. I'll splash some cold water on my face and then go back and mingle. Observe. Try to slip in questions.

But the bathroom is occupied, and Carly's just taking a spot outside the door.

From behind it I hear a sound. Like choking. Or maybe sobbing.

"Who's in there?" I whisper to Carly.

"Sam."

"She must be really upset. It sounds like she's crying."

"Really? That's what you think it sounds like?" Carly raises an eyebrow, not moving from where she leans against the wall. I realize she's not quite sober. "How do you think she stays so thin?"

Understanding dawns. "Oh." Sam's not sobbing—she's throwing up. She's bulimic.

"My brother was trying to help her. Trying to get her to stop being obsessed with perfection." Carly rolls her eyes. "A lost cause."

The bathroom door opens, and I realize, too late, that the sounds inside ceased a minute ago.

Sam's high cheekbones are flushed. "Your brother," she hisses at Carly, "was the only one who tried to save me. Everyone else knew how bad things were at home, but he was the only one who cared. He even got between me and my dad once. I paid for it later, but still he stuck up for me in a way no one else ever had. But then he fell in love with Naomi, and it was like he didn't even see me anymore." Her face drops forward, and her blond hair swings over her eyes like a wing covering a sleeping bird.

"So are you saying that you hurt him?" Carly puts her hand to her mouth. "Him and Naomi?"

"Of course not." Sam raises her chin. "But back then, I thought Terry must have killed her. And you know what? I didn't care. If he had called and asked me to go away with him, I would have left in a minute. I wouldn't have hesitated. All these years, I kept my old AOL address just in case. I kept thinking he would come back for me. Terry saved me, and then he just walked out of my life and left me all alone." Her eyes glitter with unshed tears.

173

CHAPTER 36

I'M NOT ANYONE

"OH, SAM." CARLY FOLDS THE OTHER WOMAN into a hug. Leaving them to their tears, I go into the bathroom. When I come out, they're gone, but Jason's standing just outside the door.

And he's staring at me.

"What's your game?" he demands. "Why are you following me?"

"I don't know what you're talking about." Even to me, I sound unconvincing.

He takes a step closer. I step back, but there's nowhere to go. He puts his hands on either side of me so that I'm pinned against the wall.

"I saw you at the funeral, I saw you at McDonald's, and now you're here." Flecks of spit land on my face. "Did you think I wouldn't notice?"

"I, I, I . . ." The words get stuck in my throat. He's so close I can feel the heat radiating from his body. His face shines with sweat, and there are damp rings under both of his arms.

"I hear the clicks on my phone." His pupils look wide, unfocused. "I know you guys are tapping me."

"What?" I don't have to pretend to be confused.

"You've bugged my house. You've got undercovers following me."

Does he think I'm a cop or an informant? "I'm not anyone." Remembering Duncan's plan for a cover story, I add, "I'm just Duncan's girlfriend."

"Right." He rolls his eyes. "And now go run off and report to Steve. Just be sure you tell him one thing for me." He pokes a finger in my sternum. "You tell him that no matter how hard you guys try, I'll still be one step ahead of you."

He spins around, leaving me shaking. He's moving toward the front door, so I head toward the back. Has Jason just confessed to murdering my parents? Is Stephen really having him followed?

Someone is cutting through the shadowy side yard just ahead of me, underneath the oak tree. At first I think it's Duncan, but then I catch a whiff. It's Benjy, still in his dirty overcoat, his hair sticking up in spikes. We reach the group around the table at about the same time.

"Hey, Benjy." Carly pulls her lips back in an imitation smile. "How've you been doing?" Her husband puts his arm around her protectively.

"Oh, you know, they surprise you and put little needles in your scalp and listen to you for years whether you know it or not." Carly starts to respond, but Benjy continues, his words like a string of freight cars. The whole party has fallen silent, except for the shrieks of a little girl running through the sprinkler. "They have this really fantastic equipment they use to check my head, to see if the electricity is a little different. It's easier to focus, see, because of all the fillings I got." He opens his mouth and points at jumbled teeth and at gaps where teeth used to be.

"Fillings," Sam repeats. "You did go to the dentist a lot."

"Exactly," Benjy nods rapidly, as if someone finally understands him. "That wasn't a coincidence. They wanted me there."

Audrey steps toward him. "Can I make you up a plate?" Her smile is genuine, but by the way she phrases it, it's clear that she doesn't want him touching the food. And that she wants him to take whatever she gives him and go away.

I'm not sure Benjy's capable of understanding the nuances.

"Can I share some food, break the mood, be so crude?" His expression is oddly flat.

"How about if I get you a little bit of everything?" Audrey says. She's already begun filling a paper plate.

Benjy hasn't noticed me yet, and I don't want him to. Spotting Duncan, I slip behind him.

Duncan turns and whispers, "Don't worry. I see this guy all the time. He's harmless."

But Benjy catches a glimpse of me. "Naomi's here," he says.

I freeze, my stomach rising up and pressing against the bottom of my throat. Now everyone will know who I am.

"Naomi's here in spirit," Carly agrees. "Her and Terry."

But I'm not off the hook. Benjy's still staring in my direction. "Be careful, Naomi. I said who you gonna call and it's Ghostbusters." He shakes his head, his mouth twisting. "No, that came out wrong. It's a joke. But who *are* you gonna call?"

Stephen comes around the corner. "Hello, Benjy."

At the sight of him, the other man freezes.

"I need to go." Benjy takes a step back. "I'm getting very uncomfortable right now. I think somebody might be trying to shoot me."

Stephen winces and raises his empty hands. "I'm not a policeman today, Benjy. I'm just a person. You're safe."

Benjy shakes his head. "In the hills, flies are landing." He looks from face to face as if imparting some important news. "Amongst all confused the wind speaks."

He turns and snatches the half-filled plate from Audrey. With a muffled cry of surprise, she lets go. He scurries out of the yard.

"Who was that?" she says. "How did you guys know him?"

"I've seen him around," Gregg says. "You can't really miss that hair."

"He was in our year at school." Sam sighs. "He's schizophrenic. He used to be so smart. He got the highest SAT score of anyone in school. Not just our year. Any year. He got accepted into all these big-name colleges and ended up going to Stanford. But one year he came home for Christmas break and never went back. He was saying everyone was looking at him."

"The way he was acting, he was right," Carly says. "Everyone *was* looking at him. He was talking to people who weren't there and claiming that the weather guy on Channel Eight was sending him secret messages through his tie."

"I met him in the cemetery yesterday when I was walking with Nora." I step out from behind Duncan. "I heard he sits on Naomi's grave and talks to her. And then he tried to talk to me, but I didn't really understand him."

"What did he say?" Lauren asks.

"Something about halos and snow, blood and hands. And that he was sorry. It all kind of ran together and didn't make much sense. The only thing I really remember was he said, 'Orange trucks suffer.'"

Carly puts her hand to her chest. "Oh my God. Terry's truck was orange."

"Was that the Christmas when he started going crazy?" Sam asks the group.

By the looks on their faces, it was.

Stephen looks thoughtful. "We were both volunteers for search and rescue back then. After Naomi's body was found, we got called out to help search for evidence, but Ben was pretty worthless. He kept wandering around and talking to himself."

"Oh my God." Carly's eyes are wide. "He could have gone crazy because he killed them. Because he killed my brother and Naomi."

"Whoa, Carly, whoa!" Stephen raises his hands. "Of course, we'll bring Ben in for questioning. But just because someone is mentally ill doesn't mean they're violent. Most schizophrenics are only a danger to themselves. We've never had any complaints about Ben being violent. Drinking in public, trespassing—it's all misdemeanors."

"Come off it." Carly clenches her fists. "It makes perfect sense. He must have gone with them that day. The only kind of person who would stab Naomi so many times is a crazy person." Other people nod. Her husband pulls her closer.

"Carly," Sam says, "this is Ben we're talking about. If he did it, he wasn't capable of keeping it a secret back then. And he sure isn't capable of keeping one now."

"He could be talking about it all the time, for all we know," Sam points out. "Who hears what Ben's trying to say? Nobody wants to get too near him. Nobody wants to pay attention. He could have been trying to tell us the truth all along."

CHAPTER 37

HEALED-OVER SCAR

WHEN I REACH THE TURNOFF FOR THE forest, I push the button on my car's odometer. Of course, it's not precise, and it was never meant to be, but several old news stories mentioned that my mom's body was found two miles from here.

And that's where I'm going. To the part of the woods where my parents took their final breaths. The place where we were last together as a family.

I know it won't look the same. For one thing, it's summer, not winter. But with all the dreams I've been having, maybe things are coming back, the way Quinn said they would. Being in the woods might spark more memories, or at least more dreams.

Last night, Duncan offered to walk me home from his parents' party, but I said no. I didn't need any distractions, like both of us thinking about that kiss. Before I left, I told Duncan what Jason had said, his paranoid accusations. Did Jason know about my dad's money because he took it? Was his face the last one my parents saw?

Of course, it's still possible Benjy did it. Nora loves him, but I have a feeling Nora loves everyone.

When the odometer clicks to 2.0, I find a wide spot in the road, pull over, and park. My bare thighs stick to the vinyl seat as I slide out. Since I don't own hiking boots, I'm wearing tennis shoes. From the backseat, I grab my pack. Inside are an apple, a bottle of water filled from the tap, printouts of news stories, and some screenshots from both *America's Most Wanted* and the recent stories about my dad's jawbone being found. Anything that shows a photo of the woods.

As I pick my way through the blackberries bordering the road, I pop a berry into my mouth. It's sweet and so ripe it nearly melts on my tongue, leaving behind dozens of seeds. The next is mouth-puckeringly sour.

Under the canopy of the evergreens, it's at least ten degrees cooler, which is a relief. The ground is carpeted with pine needles dried to copper. I'm a city girl. I can recognize a discarded candy wrapper at twenty paces, but I can name only a few of the plants and trees I see around me. From my grandmother, I know the names of some wildflowers, but here it's just a million shades of green, from the bright chartreuse of the ferns to the gray-green needles hanging far overhead. Unseen birds twitter and cheep. In the distance, I hear the babble of water.

Taking a deep breath, I look around. Only a few trees are small enough to be Christmas trees. On the rest, the branches don't begin until far overhead. Most of these trees must have been here long before I was born, or my parents, or even Grandma. They started out as seedlings and then stretched themselves toward the sun, stacked branch on branch into the sky.

About the only time I've spent in the wilderness is the four days in fifth grade when we went to Outdoor School. We looked at bugs and leaves, and at night we slept in cabins crowded with bunk beds. My foster family didn't have a sleeping bag, at least not one they would let me take, so my fifth-grade teacher, Mrs. Winters, lent me one.

I thought I would be more freaked out being here, but I'm not. It's just me and the peaceful woods. So far, no ghosts.

And even though it would be nice to just stay here admiring the beauty, I need to make the ghosts come out. I look at photographs, trying to memorize the patterns of branches. The way the limbs cut the sky into triangles, how two trees share the air. Then I look back up at the real trees as I slowly walk forward. I look up and down and back and forth so much I start to feel dizzy. There are hundreds of trees here, tree after tree after tree, stretching back forever.

Every step changes what I see. It's possible I could be standing right in front of one of the trees in the photos, but the angles wouldn't match unless I was on a different side. In fact, I realize that the older photos I so carefully compiled are completely useless. Things would have grown in fourteen years. Not only grown, but branches could have been broken off, or a tree could have been hit by lightning. Nothing stays the same.

And *America's Most Wanted*—were the shows even filmed in the real locations? Or did they go to some back lot, where the same few trees stood in for every forest on every TV program, where cars crashed off the same cliff, show after show? It would certainly be cheaper, and from what I've seen on YouTube, that show never did look very slick.

This whole idea was stupid. My chest aches as if there's a stone inside, a stone so heavy it might pull me over.

No! I promised my parents' memory I would find who murdered them. I can't give up now. I close my eyes and try to remember. Try to pretend that I'm little, bundled up against the cold. Did we stop and have hot chocolate? I'm almost sure of it, can almost taste the creamy sweetness on my tongue.

And I'm rewarded, not with a memory but with a logical deduction. None of the articles said anything about snowshoes or skis, so my family must have gone only as far as I could walk on my short legs. Unless maybe one of my parents carried me. But a kid that age would weigh—what? Thirty pounds? My parents wouldn't have wanted to carry me too far, even if they took turns. And once they cut down a tree, one of them would have had to drag it, green branches sweeping the snow. So they probably stayed close to the road.

The more recent news stories might still hold a clue as to where it happened. I shuffle pages until I come to the ones about my dad's jawbone turning up in a dog's mouth. A screenshot I made from a TV news program shows a tree with a branch cut off at about head height, leaving behind a big, healed-over scar roughly two feet in diameter. The picture is too tightly focused to know what is behind it, whether it's more woods or the road or what.

I move forward, slowly scanning the trees for that

scarred place. It's not possible to walk in a straight line. I have to detour around stony outcroppings and clumps of blackberries. Confront fallen branches, some that have come to rest a few feet off the ground. Each presents a puzzle. Over or under?

I imagine this landscape covered with a white blanket of snow. Part of it stained by the blood I remembered seeing at the hypnotist's. Are my parents still part of this place? If you die, do you leave some fragment, like a ghost or a memory, behind? Or, just thinking of it in purely physical terms, are atoms from their flesh and blood and bones in the air I breathe, in the dust my tennis shoes kick up?

Something snags my attention. I turn my head to look again. It's a tree with a cut-off branch. At about head height. The healed cut is almost two feet across. I look back down at the screenshot from the recent news story, and then back up at the tree.

And that's when I find myself falling.

CHAPTER 38

SOMETHING IS COMING

THE FALLEN BRANCH SIX INCHES OFF THE ground that I just hooked my ankle on gives way with a *crack*. As I fall, my papers fly ahead of me. I barely manage to get my hands in front of my face. Time slows down. My palms skid along the duff. My chest hits the ground, knocking the air out of me, and then my front teeth meet the dirt. They waver but decide to stay put as grit fills my mouth. Finally, I'm still. I lever myself up on my elbows and spit out the dirt, wipe my lips with the back of one hand.

Rolling to my hands and knees, I begin to push myself up onto my right foot. Gingerly, I put weight on my bad left foot. But when I try to take a step, the pain gets a million times worse, and I crumple to the ground. My left ankle feels like it's on fire.

It's sprained, at a minimum. Wincing, I pull off my shoe and sock. I don't see any bones sticking out or obvious bumps where there didn't used to be bumps. And I can wiggle my toes, if that means anything. But the little hollow under my anklebone is already starting to look puffy.

There's an acronym for treating injuries, and after a few seconds I remember it. RICE: rest, ice, compression, elevation.

With a hiss, I prop my bare foot up on what's left of the branch that caused this whole mess. That covers rest and elevation. I don't have any ice. I don't have anything to compress my ankle with. I can only do half of the four things you're supposed to do.

Nothing around me but trees. I can't be that far from the road, but I'm not exactly sure where it is.

What an idiot I am! I dig out my cell phone to call 911. Soon the rescue workers will be standing over me, rolling their eyes.

But my phone says NO SERVICE. I hold it at arm's length, try pointing it in different directions. For one second the display wavers, as if it's on the verge of giving me a weak signal, but then it settles back down to NO SERVICE.

I take stock. No one—not Nora or even Duncan—knows where I am. And I'm not due at Fred Meyer until the day after tomorrow. If I don't show up, my manager and coworkers will probably just shrug, at least for a day or two.

I've got that twelve-ounce bottle of water, but how long will it last? I'm not even sure I filled it to the top. How much liquid is in an apple? How many days can you go without water? Is it three? Is it less if it's hot?

If I stay here and wait for someone to find me, will it be too late?

When I first walked under the trees, the shade was not

186

that much cooler than it had been in the open. But I'm starting to shiver. It must be shock. I didn't even put a sweater in my backpack. It was ninety-seven degrees when I left, hot enough that I couldn't even imagine a world in which I might want a sweater. Medford is always hotter than Portland.

Hotter during the day, but colder at night. The temperature tonight will probably be in the forties. Since I'm higher up, maybe even colder. And I'm wearing only a T-shirt and cutoff jeans. A hot drop falls on my thigh, and I realize I'm crying. Which is stupid, because I need the liquid.

But this is ridiculous. I can't be that far—no more than a mile, and I suspect much less—from where I parked my car. I didn't see any other cars on the access road, but people must drive down it. Even if they don't, it's only two miles from the main road.

Surely I can crawl back to my car. Or at least to an open spot in the trees, where I might be able to make that flicker in my cell phone turn into a single bar.

I carefully lift my foot and, biting my lip, put on my sock and then my shoe, leaving it unlaced. My ankle is definitely swelling. I flip over and, with my bad foot raised, crawl forward in the direction I came from. It's hard going. A twig gouges my palm. A rock scrapes my knee. I'm trying to maneuver on four unpadded, unprotected surfaces. Maybe I can find a fallen branch sturdy enough to use as a cane.

As I scan the ground, I spot something right in front of me. And it's not a branch. It's small and weathered gray. The color of a stone.

But it's not a stone.

Everything goes still. I don't want to pick it up, but I do.

It's not very heavy. It's not a twig.

I think it's a bone.

I remember a book I read about people hunting dinosaur fossils in Montana. The problem is that old bones really do look just like rocks. The book said the way to tell them apart is by licking. If it sticks to your tongue, then it's a bone, because bones are porous.

I wipe my find on my shirt, wipe it and wipe it until it's as clean as it's going to get. Then I stick out my tongue and touch just the tip to the surface.

And it sticks.

I yank it away, my stomach rising. I spit and keep spitting—never mind needing to conserve body water.

It could be an animal bone. It must be. I cradle it in my palm. It's smaller at the top, flares out at the bottom. Both ends are squared off. I hold it next to my fingers.

I think it's a finger bone.

From the same hand that once held mine, that lifted me high in the air, that surely brushed the hair back from my forehead? Is that what I hold loose in my hand? Is that what I pressed against my mouth?

No. Other animals must have bones like this. I run through the possibilities. Deer have hooves. Skunks are too small. Raccoons' hands wouldn't be this big.

Maybe a bear?

And just as I think *bear*, the birds stop singing.

Something is coming. Crashing through the underbrush.

CHAPTER 39

FRECKLED WITH RED

MY HEART POUNDS IN MY EARS. SOMETHING big is out here in the woods with me. It's coming closer. And I'm hurt and can't run away. Ignoring the pain, I press myself to the ground, still as a rabbit.

But wouldn't a bear or any other animal be less, I don't know, less noisy? One with nature? I realize I'm being ridiculous. Whatever is moving through the woods must be a person.

"Help!" I shout. "Can someone help me?" My voice is weak. I feel stupid, like a little kid playing a prank.

"Hello?" a man shouts back, surprise coloring his voice.

"Can you help me? I'm hurt!"

A few seconds later, Stephen Spaulding walks into view. The chief of police who was trying to get everyone to calm down yesterday so they wouldn't form a lynch mob and go after Benjy.

"Hello! It's Olivia, isn't it? What's wrong?" He's

scanning me from head to toe, and then his gaze sharpens as he sees my unlaced shoe. "Your ankle?"

"I was hiking. I might have broken it."

He comes closer and drops to his knees. "Okay if I touch it?"

"Yeah."

As he gently pulls off my shoe and sock, my shoulders relax. Even though his cool fingers leave hot pain trailing behind as he pokes and twists, it's nothing compared with the fear that was devouring me.

"I was worried you were a bear," I say. Part of it comes out as a squeak as he moves my foot.

He laughs. "A bear! Bears are usually more scared of you than you are of them." He starts putting my sock and shoe back on, and even though he's careful, I suck in my breath. "I'm pretty sure your ankle's sprained, not broken. Of course, you'll need to get an X-ray." He returns his gaze to my face. "Was that your car I saw when I drove in here?"

I nod.

He tilts his head. "Kind of a weird spot to pick to go hiking. There are no marked trails around here, so it's not easy going."

"Yeah. I learned that the hard way."

He's still looking at me, waiting for an explanation. I have to give him a little more. Better to stick close to the truth.

"After hearing everyone talk about what happened to that Naomi and Terry, I decided to come out here and check it out."

He frowns. "Don't you think that's kind of morbid?" There's a burst of chatter from a microphone clipped to his shoulder. His eyes never leave my face as he reaches up and turns down the sound.

What can I say? "I don't know."

"You should realize after what happened yesterday that it's not a game to her friends and family." He shakes his head. "It's not a human-interest story to them. Two people died in these woods."

"I've just been thinking about them a lot, sir. I wasn't being disrespectful." My voice breaks a little.

His face softens, almost imperceptibly. "Okay. And call me Stephen."

"Are you here because of the case?"

He nods. "We're going to be conducting a new search because of the jawbone that was recovered in this area. If we find more bones, we might be able to figure out exactly how Terry Weeks was killed. After all these years, though, we'll be lucky to find any. Animals like to chew on them. They get splintered and pockmarked and scattered."

I push away the mental images. "I've got one for you. I think."

"Got one what?"

"A bone."

He jerks his head back. "Are you serious?"

For an answer, I hold it out, pinched between finger and thumb.

His eyes widen in amazement. Then he pulls a pair of latex gloves from his back pocket and puts them on. He holds out his palm, and I let go. I let go of my father's hand, or at least what I believe is part of it.

He catches his breath as he regards it. "Where did you find that?"

When I point, I find myself noticing my own finger, thinking about the bones beneath my flesh.

He squints, then looks back down at his palm. "It does look like a human knucklebone. Although you would be surprised how much animal bones can resemble human bones." With his free hand, he carefully takes the glove off by turning it inside out, leaving the bone trapped within. He knots the glove and then slips the makeshift holder into the front pocket of his uniform. Then he gets to his feet and walks to where I was pointing. "Is this the spot?"

"I think so."

He crouches and inspects the ground, pushing aside ferns, but finally stands up. "At least now I know where to center the search." He pulls what looks like a roll of orange tape from his pocket. But when he tears off a strip and ties it to a branch, it doesn't stick to anything, just flutters in the light breeze. He turns back. "Okay, now we need to get you to a hospital. Put your backpack on your lap. I'm going to carry you."

My face gets hot. "Maybe I could just put my arm around your shoulders and hop."

"That would take too long, and you'd probably just hurt your other ankle in the process." He's already squatting, lifting my arm and putting it around his neck, threading his own arm under my bent legs. When he stands up, I hear him trying not to grunt. I'm guessing I weigh more than he thought, but he'll never admit it.

"I swear I'm a pretty good hopper." I'm babbling, trying to ignore the fact that I am now clasped to this cop's chest. "And this time I would pay attention to where I'm going." His face seems to be getting red. "Are you sure this is okay?"

"I used to hunt around here when I was growing up. Back then I could field-dress a deer and carry it out myself on my back. Pretty sure you weigh less than a deer."

The last time I was carried through the woods, it was probably a lot easier. I would have weighed about a fifth of what I do now.

And it's now that I have a flash of memory. Of the last time I was carried through these same woods.

Only it's not my dad who's carrying me. It's not my mom.

It's someone who is holding me tight and muttering under their breath. Pressing the back of my head with the flat of a hand. My face so tight against their shoulder that I can barely breathe.

All I can see is a pair of dark boots hurrying through the snow.

Snow churned pink, freckled with red.

CHAPTER 40

LET ME GO

I FREAK OUT. THRASHING, KICKING, ARCHING
my back, grunting the word *no*—doing all the things I
was too afraid to do fourteen years ago. But I feel as if I'm
three years old again.

Stephen sets me down in a hurry. I'm flat on my back
on the ground, a rock digging painfully into my spine. But
underneath me there's dirt, not snow.

"Olivia? Are you all right? Can you hear me?"

He kneels over me, running his fingertips over my
scalp, his fingers snagging in my hair. He looks scared.

I roll onto my side and throw up. In my mind, I again
see the scarlet blood spotting the snow, feel the rough
fabric of a coat scraping my cheek, hear the voice muttering above me. My stomach convulses again, but all that
comes out is strings of bitter yellow bile.

"What just happened?" I say, more to myself than
to him.

"I think you just had a grand mal seizure. All of a sudden you went stiff, and then your arms and legs started

jerking. I'm just lucky I was able to set you down before I dropped you."

I push myself up to my elbows and then sit up.

He presses his lips together. "Your eyes were moving, but they were unfocused. Have you ever had a seizure before?"

I'm not going to tell him it wasn't that. It wasn't that at all. "No, sir—I mean, Stephen."

His mouth twists as he regards me. "I can't feel any injuries to your skull, but you must have hit your head when you fell. We need to get you to the hospital ASAP." He pronounces it ay-sap, and he's already gathering me back up, getting to his feet with a grunt. He starts walking much faster than he did before, fast enough that I'm bouncing against his torso.

"I'm already feeling better," I tell him, pushing back my memories. "I don't think anything's really wrong. It was probably just, like, shock. From finding that bone."

"Right now I don't think it's up to you or me to decide what's wrong with you," he says as we move into the open. "I'll feel a lot better after you've had an MRI or a CT scan or something."

Past his shoulder I see my car, with his cop car parked right behind. "I'm pretty sure I can drive." The Mazda is the most valuable thing I own. I don't want to leave it here to be stolen or vandalized.

"No way." Stephen half rests me on the hood of his car while he digs for his keys.

"It's not like my ankle's broken. It's just I can't put my full weight on my foot, that's all. My car's an automatic, so I don't even need my left foot. And I promise"—mentally, I

195

cross my fingers—"that I'll drive straight to the hospital." I'm pretty sure it's a $250 copay for an emergency-room visit. Probably a bunch more if it involves a CT scan or an MRI.

"And I would be liable if you ended up plowing through a light because your foot decided not to cooperate or you had another seizure. I can see the headlines now. 'Police chief abandons injured girl in woods.'" He opens the door to the back of the police car and plops me down on the hard seat. I hiss a little as my ankle brushes against him. "See if you can put your leg up and still get a seat belt on."

I turn sideways. The seats are formed with weird dips that I realize are shaped like the prisoners who must normally ride back here. There are indentations for their butts and shoulders and heads. But I manage to stretch out my leg and still buckle up as Stephen watches, shaking out his arms and massaging his biceps. He no longer seems like the rigid cop who would never color outside the lines. His fear for me has softened him, made him more a person than a cop.

Maybe there's a way I can use that. "So what do you think really happened with Naomi and her boyfriend?" I ask after he gets in the car and pulls out onto the road. The police radio has been turned down, but little voices drift back to me. "Do you think it was Benjy?"

"We'll interview him, sure, but in my opinion, that guy's just mentally ill. He's not a killer. You have to feel sorry for him. He was going places, but then something that wasn't his fault sent him off the rails. Yesterday, everyone was so busy pointing fingers, but there's a strong

196

possibility it was actually a serial killer." We're already on the main road.

"A serial killer?"

"About a year after the couple died, a girl in Grants Pass was murdered. Stabbed to death. She had long dark hair, just like Naomi's. Sometimes the first crime in a series is worked as a single case and then closed, and no one realizes it's related until years later."

He's talking about Angie Paginini. "Wouldn't there be more than just one or two girls if it was a serial killer?"

"Not if the killer kept moving." Stephen's hair is cut so close I can see the little white dots of his scalp between the bristles. His eyes never leave the road. "If you kill someone in one state and then kill someone else in a different state, chances are pretty good no one will ever put the two murders together, especially if you don't leave evidence like shell casings or fingerprints or DNA behind."

"Jason's a trucker," I say. "That means he's always moving on." I decide not to mention what I know about the FBI task force.

"Jason Collins?" He shakes his head and makes a sound like a laugh. "I don't think so."

"He said some weird stuff to me last night. About how people are tapping his phones. And about how you're watching him."

In the rearview mirror, I see Stephen's eyes widen. "Who? Did he mean me? That I'm watching him?"

"Yeah."

"Hmm." He looks thoughtful. "Of course, we're going to be reinterviewing Jason along with everyone else who was a friend of Naomi or Terry. We're following up all possible leads. But my money's still on it being a stranger."

"But why? Why would someone just randomly kill people?" My stomach clenches. How can you ever let down your guard if there are monsters walking around who look like people?

He sighs. "Some people enjoy killing. They don't have any more reason than that. Thankfully, it's a very small percentage of the population."

"But why kill a couple?" I shift on the hard seat. "Don't serial killers usually kill either all men or all women?"

"It could be he killed Naomi and then killed Terry when he realized she wasn't alone. And some killers are jealous of people who are capable of forming relationships, so they'll target couples."

Like the couple on the Northern California beach that Duncan told me about. "But whoever killed her and that Terry guy took their car," I protest. "And Naomi's kid."

"Boy, you really have been reading up on it." Even though he doesn't have his lights or sirens on, Stephen is still driving about ten miles an hour over the speed limit, his hands tight on the steering wheel. I wish I could reassure him about my "seizure" without telling him the truth. "Anyway, the two still might be related. He didn't keep the truck. Maybe he only took it so he could easily transport the kid."

"But why didn't this guy just kill the kid?"

He looks pained. "Even a serial killer might balk at killing a toddler."

I realize that it's more than that they simply couldn't bring themselves to kill a little kid. They still could have left me there in the cold woods with the bodies of my parents. They could have walked away and let chance decide whether I died from exposure or whether some other person venturing out in the wintry forest found me in time.

But instead they took me somewhere safe, a place where they knew I would be found. And then they let me go.

CHAPTER 41

LIKE I NEVER WAS

ALL DAY AT WORK, I'VE HAD TO ANSWER questions about my blue plastic walking boot. My ankle's not even broken, just sprained, but the doctor wants me to wear the boot for ten days as my ligaments heal. After I was done at the hospital—I was able to talk them out of doing a scan of my head—Duncan picked me up in his mom's car and drove me to get the Mazda.

We talked a lot. He told me that he wants to be my friend more than he wants to be my boyfriend. I'm not sure he was totally telling the truth, but my truth is that I missed him. Plus I still need someone to help me figure out what really happened to my parents.

The only two good things about the boot are that it's on my left foot, so I can still drive, and that it allows me to work, because I can't afford to take time off. The bad news is it attracts a lot of attention, mostly from customers who want to tell me about the times they've sprained their own ankles. In detail.

The vinyl seat scorches me when I get into my car.

Nora asked me to bring back some lemonade, but when I pull into my driveway, I see a cop car parked in front of her house. Her curtains twitch, and then Stephen steps out of her door, dressed in uniform, face flushed from the heat. "Just the person I came to visit," he says, meeting me halfway down the walkway. "I wanted to see how your ankle was holding up. And I need your help to plan the new search."

"Just a sec." I hold out the sweating bottle. "I'm going to run in and give this to Nora."

He shakes his head. "I was just visiting with her, but she said she wasn't feeling well. She's taking a nap."

"She won't mind if I stick it in her fridge."

He steps in front of me, and I'm suddenly conscious of the jut of his chest, the gun on his hip. "No, Olivia. You shouldn't go in there."

The hair rises on the nape of my neck. Something is terribly wrong. I don't waste time arguing. I step to the right, then slip past him on the left, clomp up the two steps as fast as I can, and fling open the door.

Nora is sitting on the couch. Her lap is covered by a pile of afghans, and she's wearing those fake UGGs on her feet. Her head is tilted back against the cushions. Her glasses are lying on the floor.

Her eyes are open. Not moving or blinking.

"Oh my God—" I turn to Stephen, who has followed me inside, but then I see he already knows that something's wrong.

He closes the door behind him. I take a step back, but the coffee table catches me in the back of the knees.

He grabs my wrists and pulls me close. Through

gritted teeth, he says, "You asked so many questions, turned up in so many places. So I ran you through our databases. Turns out you're not who you say you are."

Inside, I'm frozen. Everything's wrong. Everything's twisted. "I don't know what you're talking about. I'm Olivia Reinhart."

"Yes. And you're also Ariel Benson. Terry and Naomi's daughter. And once I saw that, it explained why you seemed so familiar."

He looks over at Nora's still figure. "She saw me knocking on your door and invited me in. She realized I had figured out who you were. But the thing is"—his eyes flash back to mine—"she hadn't figured out who *I* was. Before she died, she said you hadn't told anyone else who you were."

"What did you do to her?"

"Her heart just stopped," he says, but I know he's lying. Or at least leaving out the part where he did something to make it stop, like put a sofa pillow over her face. "Now I need you to come with me so we get everything straightened out." He shifts his grip so that he's holding both my wrists with one hand. Before I can react, he's slapped handcuffs on me.

"What are you doing? Am I under arrest?"

"Anything you say can and will be used against you," he says, but isn't there supposed to be more to it than that?

He opens the door and makes me walk ahead of him. *Nora's dead, Nora's dead, Nora's dead* pulses in me. I clomp along, feeling as if I'm in one of my nightmares, the ones where I run and run but somehow stay in the same place. The neighborhood is deserted, everyone at work. The few people who might be home are probably hunkered down in the air-conditioning with the curtains drawn.

At his cruiser, he opens the door on the back passenger side.

This time, instead of easing me in, he pushes me into the seat and doesn't bother to tell me to use the seat belt. The windows are tinted, and there's no chance anyone will see me tucked back in the recessed space. Maybe I can jump out when the car is moving? As he closes the door, I reach forward and grab the handle with one of my cuffed hands. It doesn't open.

He gets in the driver's seat, slams the door, and starts driving. Fast.

The doubling thing is happening again. Just like fourteen years ago, I'm staring at the floor of a car. There's no bloody knife, but the muttering voice is familiar.

"What the hell just happened?" he says, but not to me. "How did you let it go this far, Stephen? You're a good husband, a good father, and a good cop. But then she had to come around asking questions. Trying to connect the dots. She didn't give you any choice. Just like her parents." His voice is equal parts anguished and angry.

I raise my cuffed hands so I can touch Nora's necklace. It feels like an anchor. Like the only bit of goodness in this car. My eyes fill with tears, but I blink them back. I can't afford to fall apart now.

Where is he taking me? Because I'm pretty sure it's not to the police station. From between the two front seats, tiny, tinny voices drift up. Can I get to the radio somehow and call for help? But could I ever get the person on the other end to believe me?

My phone is in my back pocket, and he hasn't taken it from me—yet.

"So what really happened to my parents?"

He hesitates, but then the words rush from him as if they have been dammed up for years. "First, you have to understand what was going on back then. My dad had been sick forever. Cancer. And then he died. The economy sucked. My mom couldn't get a job. I was living at home, going to community college, making a few bucks doing yard work. Me and my mom and my little sisters were living off what we could get from the church pantry, and half the time the shelves were bare. Deer season was over, but my sisters were crying from hunger. They needed to eat. So I took my rifle and I went out into the woods. I saw a deer moving through the trees. I swear to God, I didn't see a person. I saw a deer, the flick of its white tail. So I shot it. But—but when I took out my knife and went to gut it, I found Terry. Terry Weeks. And he was dead. Wearing these stupid white gloves that Naomi must have made him. And I'd killed him."

Thoughts tangle and collide in my head. Now I know the truth. This man who is only a few feet from me has killed three people I loved. My mom and dad, and now Nora. I want to scream and shout and rage. I want to punch through the Plexiglas that separates us, slide the handcuffs over his head and strangle him. But I push back the anger and the tears and the fear. There will be time for all those later—if I live.

I force myself to speak calmly. "Couldn't you have just turned yourself in and explained?" While his attention focused on his memories, I try to move my cuffed hands around to my back pocket.

"Explained what?" He makes a sound like a laugh. "That I was hunting out of season? That I had just killed a guy? I already wanted to be a cop, but shooting Terry meant that would never happen. Shooting Terry meant my life was over. I was still in shock when I heard Naomi calling for him. She came around a tree and found me with my rifle over my shoulder and my knife in my hand. I tried to explain to her it was an accident, but she went crazy, hitting me and screaming. I only meant to push her away. That's all."

My lips curl back. The emotion I've been holding at bay starts to leak out. "Push her away? You stabbed her nineteen times."

Through the Plexiglas, I see him shake his head. "I just wanted her to be quiet, to leave me alone so I could think. But she wouldn't stop fighting, stop screaming. I didn't have any other choice. She even tried to take the knife away from me."

"Yeah, to stop you from killing her!" I strain, my shoulder twisting. My fingertips brush the top of my phone.

His eyes meet mine in the rearview mirror, and I stop moving. "It was already too late. I couldn't make it better. I couldn't bring Terry back to life. It was Naomi or me. There weren't any other choices. But it was the hardest thing." His voice is hoarse. "It was awful. Do you think I haven't lived with that for years? Do you think I don't have nightmares, that what happened isn't in my thoughts every day?" His voice breaks. "And then when it was over, I heard this noise. It was you, trying to run away on your little legs. I hadn't even noticed you until then."

"Did you think about killing me?" The tears are falling from my eyes now, disobeying me.

"No," he says, but I hear the lie in his voice. "No," he repeats more softly. "How could I do that? You weren't much younger than my little sister. I could have left you there, and you would have frozen to death. But I kept you safe. I didn't touch a hair on your head. Because of my sisters, I knew how to talk to little girls. I got close and then grabbed you up, carried you to Terry's pickup, and put you inside. Then I went back to get his keys, but the first pocket I looked in was full of money. I had no idea where it had come from, but I took it and hoped people would think it explained things. The whole time I was patting him down, Naomi was looking right at me. I tried to close her eyes, but they wouldn't stay. I knew she couldn't see me, but it felt like she could. So I wrapped her in the tarp I had brought for the deer. Then I hightailed it out of there."

Again, his gaze meets mine in the rearview mirror. "You actually fell asleep on the drive. And when I saw the billboard for Walmart, I went there. I looked up at the light poles to make sure there weren't any cameras. I leaned over and opened the door of the truck for you. I told you your mommy and daddy were waiting for you inside. You looked at me once, and then you took off. I drove up to Portland, parked in the long-term lot, and wiped the truck down. And then I took a Greyhound back to Medford and hiked back to get my car, a few miles from where it happened. I was home by the end of the day."

I try to make sense of everything. "So was Benjy with you that day?"

"No. But he came out for the search after Naomi's body was found, and he must have seen me. I found one of Terry's hands that day, still in a stupid white glove. Animals probably dragged off the rest. I hid the hand in my pack and buried it later. Even if Ben had tried to tell someone about what he saw me do, that was also when he started talking about the FBI listening to him."

"So are you going to pin it on him now?"

He looks shocked. "Of course not. Not on him, not on Jason, not on anybody. We're looking at a drifter here. Someone who came, who killed, who moved on. Who's probably linked to old crimes in other states."

"What about me? How are you going to explain whatever you do to me?"

"What about you? Everyone knows you're impetuous. You moved down to Medford on the spur of the moment. And now you've decided to move on again."

It's going to take a lot of work to make his story fit. But he made his old story work fourteen years ago, when he wasn't the chief of police, when he didn't have access to evidence rooms and databases. So he can probably do it again.

Make me disappear like I never was.

CHAPTER 42

NO HOPE

WHEN STEPHEN FINALLY STOPS THE CAR, I recognize where we are. It's the same spot where I parked earlier. Next to the part of the forest where my parents died.

I've come full circle.

After getting out of the car, he walks to my side and opens the door. His gun is in his hand, and it's pointed right at my chest.

"Get out."

I don't have much choice. It's surprisingly hard to climb out of a car when you can't use your hands to push off.

"Now walk ahead of me." He motions with his gun toward the forest.

Imagining how the bullet will bury itself between my shoulder blades, I don't move. "You don't want to do this."

"I may not want to, but I have to." He regards me with dead eyes. "It's too late, don't you see? It was too late the minute I accidentally shot Terry all those years ago.

Everything was set in motion then. Naomi dying. Nora's heart giving out. And this."

It's now or never. Moving faster than a thought, I lean back and brace my shoulders against the frame of the car. I kick my booted foot straight out in front of me. The hard plastic goes up between his legs with every ounce of strength I can muster. He makes a sound that starts as a grunt and ends as a scream, and staggers back.

I dart past him. Suddenly, it feels as if I'm being clotheslined. He's grabbed Nora's necklace. It digs into my throat, and then with a sharp *pop*, it snaps. He tumbles to the ground behind me, groaning.

I run as fast as I can, a crazy, staggering dash made uneven because of the boot. With my hands cuffed in front of me, I can't pump my arms but have to move them in tandem. Still, fear gives me wings.

As I run, that doubling thing happens again, the past and the present overlaid. Only this time it's not a person but a place. Now I remember being little and afraid and trying to run away. Run away from a killer. The same man who will soon gather himself, get to his feet, and chase me.

Last time, he caught me. Will he do the same this time? Because I know there is no hope that he will spare me now.

My ankle protests at every step. My feet slide on the dead pine needles. Branches claw my face, poke at my eyes. Every step betrays me with a snapping twig, a stone that clacks against another. Even my own body betrays me, panting and moaning. I'm making so much noise. Is it better to be slower and quieter or to put more distance between us?

As if in answer, a bullet sings through the air past me. The sound spurs me to an even greater burst of speed.

If I can lose him, maybe I can circle back to the road, hide in the bushes, and flag down a passing car. Or move from tree to tree and follow the road back into town.

Behind me, I hear a faint thud and cry. It sounds like he fell. Tripped on a stone or a root, the way I did when we were last here. My own balance is compromised by the handcuffs and the boot. Pretty soon, I'll fall, too. I imagine him catching up, standing over me, and pulling the trigger.

I decide to seize this moment to hide and then pray he comes blundering past. On my left, the ground rises. It's covered with dry grasses, low bushes, and tall pine trees. There's no real cover. On my right, it slopes down to a thicker tangle of more bushes and blackberry vines, deep enough to hide me. I don't want to leave telltale broken canes, so I fall to my knees and tunnel into the base of a huge blackberry bush, ignoring how the thorns tattoo my face and arms with my own blood. Finally, I'm in as deep as I can get. In the shadowed darkness, I breathe shallowly. My heart is so loud that surely he'll hear it, too. Sweat traces a path down my spine.

And then I hear him, muttering and cursing. "Which way? Which way? Where did she go? You can't let her get away." He's no more than fifteen feet from me.

I close my eyes. I don't want to watch my own death come for me. I'm breathing so lightly my chest doesn't even rise a millimeter.

CHAPTER 43

NOWHERE TO RUN

JUST AS I THINK THAT HE MUST SURELY SEE me, Stephen asks himself, "What's that?" He breaks into a run. His footsteps, which were so close, now move farther away.

Even though he seems to have left, I can't risk moving too soon and giving myself away.

My dad's death was fast, but my mother must have been so frightened before she died. Had she tried to appeal to Stephen, to their long friendship? Had her disbelief at what was happening slowed her reaction? What had it been like to look into the face of someone she thought of as a friend as he stabbed her again and again? Had she thought of my father or me? Or had it all been beyond thought, a crazy struggle that lasted only a few seconds?

Tears come to my eyes as I think of her and my dad and Nora, all of them taken from me.

No! I'm not going to let it happen again. Moving as quietly as I can, I twist and strain until I can pull out my phone. When I turn it on, I see one bar. It wavers but then holds. Relief washes over me. Now to call 911 for help.

I push the 9 button, then stop. First of all, I'm going to have to risk talking. How close is Stephen? Will he hear my voice and turn back? Will he shoot me before I can finish explaining to the dispatcher what's going on?

And even if I manage to tell my story, what will the dispatcher think when I claim that the chief of police is trying to kill me? The first thing they'll probably do is check with Stephen. He'll make up a lie. It might not hold in the long run—especially once I turn up missing—but either way, I'll still be dead.

I delete the 9, put my phone on silent, and switch to my text program. Duncan's my only hope.

Nd help. Spaulding killed parents!! Took me 2 same place. Hiding from him in woods.

What? Srsly? Call police.

No! He IS police. Plz come b4 he finds me. I'll try 2 get back 2 road.

His answer comes only a second later.

Coming 4 u.

My sense of relief doesn't last long. It will still take twenty minutes for Duncan to drive here. And even before that, he's going to have to get his hands on a car. Should I stay where I am for a while longer? Try to head back to the road now? I'm just starting to think it might be time to risk leaving when a white flake floats through the blackberry canes and past my eyes. And then another one. The flakes look like snow. Which is impossible.

It's ash.

I sniff. The air smells sweet and smoky. And the forest is tinder-dry.

Pausing every few seconds to listen, I carefully back my way out of the blackberry bush. It's even more difficult than tunneling in. All the canes I pressed one way now have to be pushed the other. Without a flat-out panic numbing me to the pain, each new scratch makes me flinch, which just makes another thorn snag on a different part of my body. As the canes finally grow sparser, I cautiously peer out. My heart is thudding in my chest. I'm so afraid I'll find Stephen waiting patiently for me, but there's no sign of him.

But about the length of a football field away, a thin plume of gray smoke is rising to the sky. Even while I watch, it grows fatter. Underneath the gray, there's the orange flicker of flames. A half dozen trees are on fire. Another line of smoke rises from a new tree. Flames the color of molten gold race up another. And now I can *hear* it. A crackle that thickens to a roar.

The fire is between me and the road. And it's getting bigger every second.

I don't think this fire is an accident. Stephen has set the forest alight, hoping to drive me out or burn me down. When I was here fourteen years ago, I could have frozen to death. Now I might turn to ashes.

Maybe I can circle around it and get back to the road.

Get to Duncan. I imagine jumping into his mom's car and getting out of here.

Even in the few seconds it takes to imagine this, the forest fire is stretching out, hungry flames finding new fuel, thanks to wind-carried embers. Moving like a living thing, the fire skitters here, takes great leaps there. It flows like liquid, flames swirling and twining.

It's mesmerizing. I shake my head and start to run from the flames. Maybe I can outrace them. The air is so hot it singes the insides of my nostrils. The white ash is falling faster and faster. After a few minutes, I risk a glance behind me. It's much worse than I thought. The flames have jumped from tree to tree, so that the fire is beginning to ring me like an open mouth. It's so close now, only a few hundred feet away, and gaining on me every second with a sound like thunder.

With my head twisted around, I can't watch my feet, so when my right toe hooks on something, I fall hard, landing with my cuffed hands in my solar plexus. The air is knocked out of me. I lie there, mouth open like a fish's, my lungs empty and my diaphragm stuck.

Get up, a woman's voice says. I don't know if it's in my head or in my ear. *You have to get up, honey.*

Now, a man's voice commands.

Suddenly, the scorching, smoky air rushes back into my lungs, hot and harsh. Gasping, I roll over, push myself to my feet, and start running again. Trees pop and snap as the flames find pockets of moisture. All around me, bits of fire flicker through the air. Each is a burning leaf that blackens to a crisp in midair. Then one of them, still burning, lands a few feet ahead of me and ignites a new fire. I swerve around it. But the fire at my back is giving birth to more and more spot fires that flare up and join the mother conflagration. I'm no longer thinking of finding Duncan or avoiding Stephen. I'm not even sure what direction I'm running in. Now all I want to do is survive for a few more seconds.

I crash through dense underbrush, veering around clumps of brambles, threading between tree trunks, my eyes constantly evaluating where I can go, where I can step. The air is as hot as a kiln. My tongue feels fat and swollen against my dry lips. Pine needles and small branches begin to swirl around me as they're pulled off the ground and sucked into the firestorm at my back. When I wipe my stinging eyes, my palm comes away smeared with ash.

Something crashes past me. Two somethings. My heart stutters in my chest. Deer. A doe and a fawn, leaping so fast they barely touch the ground before they bound off again. They live here and I don't, so I follow them as flames lick the trees and orange-and-gray clouds billow to the sky.

The fire's orange-yellow glow casts my shadow ahead of me. Behind me, a tree explodes as a pocket of hidden moisture turns to steam. Splinters shoot past me. A flaming branch falls at my feet, and I leap over it like one of the deer, ignoring the sharp pain in my ankle when I land.

Through the acrid smoke, I can still dimly see them ahead of me. The deer are cutting down into what looks like a small ravine.

I risk another look behind me. A wind-fed wall of flames twenty feet tall is racing toward me, roaring like a freight train.

There is nowhere to go. Nowhere to run. The fire is coming.

And soon it will catch me.

CHAPTER 44

EMPTY EYE OF
THE GUN

*G*O! THE VOICES WHISPER. *KEEP FOLLOWING the deer.*

As I run down the steep slope after their bounding shapes, I spot what they were making for: a stream about twenty feet across. Nervously dancing back and forth, they are now standing in it, the water just past their bellies.

My back feels like it's already on fire. The sound of the conflagration is so loud it's more a sensation than a sound, like a giant hand pushing me forward.

I leap into the water. Right before my head goes under, I snatch one final breath of scorching air. I keep my eyes open. Around me, burning branches hit the water. The legs of one of the deer churn past. Above me, there's an eerie glow, brighter than any hell I've ever imagined, as the wall of flames reaches us. I curl into a ball and will myself not to float. Will myself not to breathe as the fire roars over us.

But finally I have to. Yanking my wet T-shirt over my mouth, I pray the fabric will somehow protect my lungs from the hot gases. I put my feet under me and, with my shoulders rounded, stand up just enough that my mouth clears the water. Immediately my T-shirt dries out and then crisps on my back. Hot ash freckles my neck. I smell the sweet stench of burning hair. I suck in a breath and sink again, but the water seems lower. Has it boiled away at the edges, turned to steam?

I don't know how many times I repeat this—holding my breath until my lungs burn like the air above me— until I think it might be safe to stay on my feet. I swipe the water from my eyes and look around. A few hundred feet ahead, the fire is working its way up a slope. It's so bright I have to squint to look at it.

Around me, what had been lush forest just an hour ago has been transformed into a nightmare lunar land-scape, blackened and charred. A few trees still have burn-ing branches, while others have been reduced to limbless trunks like blackened telephone poles.

Smoke clings to the ground, low enough that even just standing up, I'm out of the worst of it.

Amazingly, the deer have survived, too, although their flanks are dotted with burned patches. A look passes between me and the mama deer, a look beyond words, but still filled with understanding.

I start to laugh. I'm alive. I'm still alive.

The mama deer looks over my shoulder at something behind me. Her ears flick forward.

"Well, hello there," a man says.

His voice is a kick to the gut. I turn around. It's Stephen Spaulding. Half his hair is gone. Burned off. And that side of his face is red and black from a terrible burn that's closed one eye. But he's still got his gun, and now he aims it at me, steadying it with his other hand.

Get back under. I fall more than dive back into the stream. Bullets stitch the water. One of my foster families liked to watch *MythBusters*, and thanks to that show I know bullets can't go very far in water. The problem is, I can't remember the exact distance. Eighteen inches? Two feet? Whatever it is, I need to stay lower than that.

I want to swim away, but with my cuffed hands, about the best I can do is pull myself forward underwater, grabbing at stones, most of which are yanked free from the muck. If I get to my feet, or even raise my head to breathe, he'll shoot me. If he gets impatient, he can just wade into the creek, pull me up like some huge fish, and put the nose of his gun against my head.

But I can't stay under the surface forever. Once more, I'm forced to raise my head to breathe. This time, I keep moving away from him, even though it means I have my back to him. With the water fighting me at every step, I try to zigzag, hoping he won't be able to aim.

I suck in a panting breath, ready to dive back under. A terrible groaning sound fills the air. It's like no sound I've ever heard. I turn. It's the deer. The mama deer. I can see the neat dark hole in her throat. He's shot her.

"No!" I scream for the first time. I reach out as if to put my hand over the hole, as if I can stop the blood, as red and shiny as paint, that begins to fountain out, but she's thrashing, going down. Her fawn watches, skittering back and forth.

"Olivia!"

At the sound of Duncan's shout, I turn. But I can't see him, just Stephen and the blackened landscape.

"Here!" I scream, my voice cracking from the smoke. "I'm over here! In the stream."

Stephen's distracted now, his gun swinging between me and the direction from which Duncan's voice came. Above him, a tree now reduced to a blackened skeleton still has one huge limb burning.

"Duncan, be careful!" I shout. I'm moving downstream, trying to put more distance between me and Stephen as well as get closer to Duncan. "Stephen's here, and he's got a gun!"

The landscape is as black as a nightmare. When Duncan appears, he's the only splash of color in it. He's running flat out, a rifle in both hands.

Stephen raises his own gun.

"Watch out!" I scream at Duncan. "He's—"

My warning is cut short by a shot.

Red blooms on Duncan's chest. He falls so hard he somersaults forward, a broken boy, and then lies unmoving in an awkward sprawl. My scream is caught in my throat.

Stephen Spaulding turns toward me, ready to complete his circle of death. The circle that has been drawn around nearly everyone I love: my father, my mother, Nora, and Duncan. And now he will add me.

Above him, that one remaining limb begins to creak as the fire eats through it. Starts to move. But Stephen only has eyes and ears for me. As fast as I can, I move to my left. He matches me step for step as he steadies his hand.

I stare straight into the round, empty eye of the gun.

Just as the limb snaps off, still on fire, and crashes into him.

CHAPTER 45

I'M READY

I'M ON MY BACK, MY ARMS AND LEGS TIED *up, unable to move. Stephen Spaulding stands over me, his gun aimed at my chest, a dead smile on his face. I buck and scream, but I can't get away. Fire licks at my face. When I focus on him again, he's holding a knife. Behind him lie the bloody bodies of my parents, of Nora and Duncan. I start to howl.*

"Easy, easy! Olivia, you're okay."

With a start, I open my eyes. I'm lying on a white bed. A middle-aged woman is leaning over me, her hand on my shoulder. She wears a badge on her black short-sleeved shirt, which has gold crosses on the collar points. A man stands behind her. He's dressed in a suit, with a badge on his belt. They're cops.

Just like Stephen Spaulding.

I shriek and try to push her away. But I only raise my arms a few inches before they stop with a jerk. Padded straps encircle my wrists and ankles. Panic squeezes me tight. How long until Stephen comes in and finishes what he started? My eyes dart around the room. Besides the two cops, there's only a table heaped with cards and stuffed animals, balloons and bouquets. No sign of him. Yet.

"Shh, shh, you're okay, Olivia," the woman says. She pats the air with empty hands.

"Where's Duncan?" My heart constricts. Is he even alive? I remember hearing the shot, seeing him fall.

"He's down the hall. He just got out of surgery, so we haven't had a chance to talk to him yet."

"So we're both under arrest?"

"Arrest?" She gives me a reassuring smile as she shakes her head. "No, Olivia, this is a hospital. I'm Chaplain Steves, and this is Detective Elemon." The man nods. "We're with the Medford police."

I raise my hands until the restraints catch them. "But if I'm not in trouble, why am I tied up?"

"The nurses did that," Chaplain Steves says. "They said you kept pulling out your IV lines and running down the hall, screaming. They had to restrain you to keep you from hurting yourself."

I hadn't noticed them until now, but slender plastic tubes run from IV bags dangling from a silver pole and then disappear under a bandage on the back of my left hand. "What's wrong with me?" My hands and arms are peppered with dozens of tiny red burns and larger yellow blisters.

"According to your doctors, you're actually doing surprisingly well, considering you just survived a forest fire. You've got some first-degree burns and a few second-degree." She touches her own short, straight hair. "And I'm afraid a lot of your hair got burned off. But the doctors were mostly worried about smoke inhalation. They want to make sure your lungs don't suddenly start filling up with fluid. They said when that happens, there's not much time to reverse it. That's why you're here in the hospital." She gives me a half smile. "Since you weren't exactly cooperating, they gave you something to sedate you."

I can still feel the drugs in my system, making my thoughts sluggish, blurring the line between past and present, reality and nightmare.

"What about Duncan?" The horror of what I saw runs through me again. "Stephen shot him!"

"I'm not a doctor, but it sounds like he'll be okay. He has a through-and-through wound on his shoulder, and some burns from falling after he was shot."

I sag back on the bed in relief.

"And if you're wondering where Chief"—she corrects herself—"I mean, Mr. Spaulding is, he's in a burn unit at a different hospital. We don't know if he'll make it. The firefighters spotted the two cars and went searching for you. It was his shooting at you and Duncan that helped them find you."

Detective Elemon speaks for the first time. "The reason we're here, Olivia, is that Spaulding told the doctor on the chopper that he was guilty of three murders. And at that point, he knew that both you and Duncan were alive, so he couldn't have meant either of you." He presses his lips together and gives his head a little shake, as if he still can't believe it. "He passed out before he could say anything more. But that's one of the reasons we want to talk to you."

I reflexively raise one hand toward my neck, where Nora's necklace should be, but the restraints won't even allow that much movement. "One of the people he killed was Nora. Nora Murdoch. I think he put a pillow over her face." Tears prick my eyes as her loss hits me again. When I blink, they run down my cheeks, and I can't even wipe them away. But for once, I don't care that people know what I'm feeling.

The chaplain's eyes widen. "Nora Murdoch? Are you sure? I heard she died, but they thought she had a heart attack."

"No. He killed her because she knew who I really was."

"Who you really are?" Detective Elemon echoes, looking puzzled. "Aren't you Olivia Reinhart?"

I take a deep breath. "My real name is Ariel Benson. And my parents are the other two people Stephen Spaulding killed."

A REAL FAMILY

"I NEED ONE MORE PIECE OF TAPE." I MEASURE with my eyes. "About ten inches long."

Duncan tears off a strip of blue painter's tape. On my knees, I wrap it along the baseboard around the corner from the hall to the living room. We're getting ready to paint the walls, but the exact same color they used to be. I brought a chip of paint into Home Depot, and they were able to match the color.

I'm living up to my end of the deal with Richard Lee. Maybe I could hire a lawyer and try to get official ownership of the house before I turn eighteen, but I figure the total cost would be far more than the 7 percent I'm paying Lee Realty.

The new paint will cover up the squares where pictures used to hang. But I plan to leave a small part of the wall untouched: the faint pencil marks my grandma made when she measured my height.

At first, I wanted to make the house look exactly the way I remembered it from when I was seven. I wanted to buy a blue teapot to set on the corner shelf, to put a TV in the old spot, to find flowered bedspreads like the ones that used to cover the beds. But then I realized I was trying to mimic the taste of a fifty-six-year-old woman. And as great as my grandmother was, that's not who I am. I'm not my grandmother; I'm not my mom; I'm not my dad. I'm me. Parts of them are in me, but I'm my own person.

I did say yes to Nora's kids when they offered me some of her furniture. I've got her coffee table and her gold brocade wingback chair with the carved wooden feet gripping balls. Hundreds came to her funeral, including people who only recognized her from the picture in the newspaper obituary. One was the lady whose dog Nora had mesmerized in the cemetery.

She may have been ready to go, but I wasn't ready to let her. The reality of her death still washes over me like a wave, or like the wildfire as it passed over me. Grief is a strange thing. You can feel it coming, and then it hits and it's all you can do to keep breathing. But eventually it passes, and you pick yourself up and start moving again. Now when I go to the cemetery, I visit Nora's grave, too. She was buried in Odd Fellows, not far from my grandma and my mom.

I've been spending a lot of time with Aunt Carly; her husband, Tim; and Lauren, who's now both my cousin and my friend. Sometimes when we're doing things together, people will ask if we're sisters. Carly floated the idea of my living with them. But even though it's amazing to have a real family again, I'm also used to being independent. So I'm staying here.

"Okay," I say, "I guess it's time to start putting down the plastic sheeting."

Duncan uses his good hand to help me to my feet, but instead of reaching for the rolls of plastic, he pulls me into a kiss that tastes like coffee and cinnamon.

Eventually, I step back. "If we keep going like this, the painting is never going to get done."

He gives me a crooked grin. "Do you have a problem with that?"

For an answer, I kiss him again.

I'm out of my boot, and Duncan's shoulder is healing, although he's going to be left with a wicked scar. Oddly, it looks something like the scar on my palm, only bigger. Both of us are freckled with little pink marks from burns, but the doctor said if we're good about using sunscreen, they should fade. Duncan didn't burn his feet, although he did melt the soles of his shoes running through the freshly burned landscape while trying to get to me. Even though he had brought his dad's hunting rifle, it didn't have any ammunition. His plan, such as it was, had been to scare Stephen with the rifle. It had worked almost too well.

Stephen's still being treated in a burn unit, but he's going to live. The district attorney told us that Stephen plans to plead guilty to all of it: killing my parents and Nora and trying to kill us. It sounds as though he will go to prison for the rest of his life.

Jason Collins has also been arrested, but not for murder. He's been dealing—and using—meth. It turns out that some truckers use it so they can stay awake and drive longer distances.

Duncan's just started back in school. Since I don't want to work at Fred Meyer forever, I'm planning on going to winter term at the community college. He says it's not fair that I can start college before him when I'm two months younger.

When we pull apart, Duncan's finger catches on my button necklace. Detective Elemon found part of it next to Stephen's car, and later Carly drove back to the same spot and picked up every single button she could find and restrung it for me. It's not quite the same, but then nothing ever is, is it?

"I guess we'd better get back to work," I tell Duncan.

"Okay." He kisses me on the nose. "Whatever you say, Ariel."

ACKNOWLEDGMENTS

Thanks to Kayla W. for helping me understand what it's like to grow up in foster care; Jake Keller of Multnomah County Sheriff's Office Search and Rescue for explaining how to tell if what you've found in the forest is a human bone; Leslie Budewitz, a mystery author with a blog on the law and fiction, for detailing what would happen to the inheritance of a minor in foster care; and Holly Hertel, a Jackson County reference librarian, for describing the library's microfilm offerings.

I'm the luckiest girl in the world because this is my twentieth book with my agent Wendy Schmalz, and my sixth with editor Christy Ottaviano. Other wonderful folks at Henry Holt include April Ward, Jessica Anderson, Christine Ma, Molly Brouillette, Kathryn Little, Lucy Del Priore, Katie Halata, Holly Hunnicutt, Allison Verost, and Angus Killick.

GOFISH

APRIL HENRY

© Randy Patten

What did you want to be when you grew up?
An ophthalmologist. Why? I have no idea. Maybe because it's so hard to spell.

When did you realize you wanted to be a writer?
Initially I thought about being a writer when I was nine or ten. Then I lost my courage and didn't find it again until I was about thirty.

What's your most embarrassing childhood memory?
People used to call me Ape, and I did a pretty good monkey impression. The trick is to put your tongue under your upper lip and scrunch up your nose while making chimp noises. Only now, looking back on it, I'm embarrassed to think about it.

What's your favorite childhood memory?
When I was ten, I asked for nothing but books for

Christmas. After we unwrapped our presents, I went back into bed and read.

As a young person, who did you look up to most?
Roald Dahl, who wrote *Charlie and the Chocolate Factory*. I wrote him letters and sent him stories, and he sent me back a couple of postcards. I still have one that complimented my story about a six-foot-tall frog named Herman who loved peanut butter.

What was your favorite thing about school?
English and math, but I liked nearly all subjects. If life were like school, I would be a millionaire. Unfortunately for my bank account, real life and school only overlap to a certain extent.

What was your least favorite thing about school?
PE. I was the clumsiest person imaginable. I hurt my knee on the pommel horse, bruised my inner arm from wrist to elbow in archery, and sank when I was supposed to be swimming.

What were your hobbies as a kid? What are your hobbies now?
I read or hung out with my friends. We lived near a cool old cemetery, and sometimes we would even go sledding or picnic there.

Now I run, read, and practice kajukenbo, a mixed marital art. We even spar—and I'm pretty good. If only my old PE teacher, Miss Fronk, could see me now.

What was your first job, and what was your "worst" job?

My first job was at a library in the children's section. I used to hide in the stacks and read Judy Blume when I was supposed to be shelving books.

My worst job was at a bank. A monkey who knew the alphabet could have done that job—and would probably have had a better time.

How did you celebrate publishing your first book?

I stink at celebrating. I did buy a pair of earrings.

Where do you write your books?

On my couch, at the coffee shop, in the library, at the car fix-it place (where I am a lot).

What do you think is the biggest challenge for a person pretending to be somebody else in order to ensure their own safety?

A couple of years ago, I attended a class taught by William Queen, who spent nearly three years undercover with the Mongols (a violent outlaw motorcycle gang). I've also read several memoirs by people who have gone deep undercover for long periods of time. Queen and the others all say the same thing: The most difficult issue is that you tend to start having divided loyalties. If you spend a lot of time with people, even if they are doing things that go against your principles, you start to like some of them. In turn, they start to like and trust you. But you can't afford to trust them, because it's likely you would be killed if they found out who you really are.

What would you do if you discovered evidence that went against the official rulings on a criminal case in your community?

It would depend on the type of evidence. If it's physical evidence, the police have chain-of-custody rules for a reason. You would have to show that this new evidence hadn't been tampered with. And if the evidence is someone's memory, well, memories can be and often are fallible.

You would also have to think about who would be willing to consider the evidence. Ideally that would be an official authority, but some people will never accept evidence that counters their view of what happened, even if (maybe especially if) their view is actually wrong. If you couldn't get anywhere with the authorities or if you were sure they wouldn't listen, then another alternative would be to find a reporter willing to break the story.

And of course you should consider if there are people out there willing to do whatever it takes to suppress the evidence.

What was your favorite part of the research you did for this book?

I knew that at the end of the book I wanted Olivia to be chased by her parents' killer through the very forest where they had died. And that she would be handcuffed. I own several pairs of handcuffs (purchased when I was learning how to get out of them), so I drove to a park by my house that has a wooded area. Once I got to that section, I put on the handcuffs and started running. It turns out it's not that hard to run in handcuffs if you're cuffed in front. You just need to get used to moving your hands in tandem, rather than in opposition to each other.

Another funny detail from this day: Usually there is no one in that part of the park. In fact, a few times I have worried about it being too isolated. But that particular day, for whatever reason, there were a whole bunch of other runners. How was I going to explain why I was running in handcuffs?

But many people don't notice things. If you don't expect to see handcuffs on a fellow runner, you don't see them. For those few that did, I decided to just try smiling. I pasted a big happy grin on my face. I could see their puzzled expressions as they looked down at my wrists, up at my smiling face, and then back down at my wrists. And then I could watch as they decided not to ask. (I like to think that if I had seem terrified or upset, someone would have.)

After the book was done, I asked my daughter, home on Christmas break from college, if I could film her running around in the woods in handcuffs so I could use the footage in a book trailer. She obliged—she is my daughter, after all— and then I told her that the character was not only handcuffed but also wearing a bulky plastic walking boot for a sprained ankle. (You want to make things as bad as possible for your characters.) I had purchased a boot at a medical supply store, and told my daughter that I needed her to put it on along with the handcuffs and run some more.

She refused. She said it was dangerous! So I swapped clothes with her, figured out how to film my own feet and hands, put on the handcuffs and the boot, and then ran around in the woods, panting very dramatically. But you know what? My daughter was right! It is dangerous. The toe of the plastic boot caught on a root and I totally took a header—while filming the whole thing. Luckily I only hurt my pride.

CHEYENNE has finally escaped from Roy Sawyer with the help of his son, Griffin. But just before they are to go on trial to testify against his father, Griffin disappears and Cheyenne gets kidnapped—this time for the kill. Can Cheyenne save herself and find Griffin? Or was Griffin a player in the plan from the beginning?

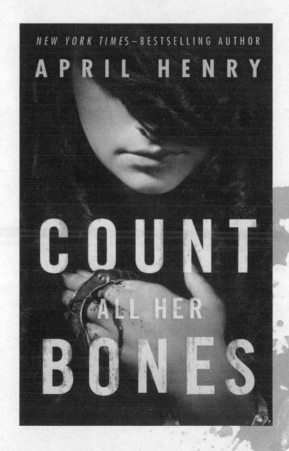

NEW YORK TIMES–BESTSELLING AUTHOR
APRIL HENRY
COUNT ALL HER BONES

KEEP READING FOR AN EXCERPT.

CHAPTER 1

THE TERROR, THE BRAVERY

CHEYENNE

"We only have ten days until the trial starts," Matthew Bennett said. "Do you feel ready?"

Cheyenne Wilder nodded. She heard the Multnomah County prosecutor sigh.

"When we're in court, please remember to answer out loud. All testimony is recorded."

"Okay." Cheyenne swallowed. Even though this was just practice in Mr. Bennett's office, her tongue felt too big for her mouth. What was it going to be like in the witness stand in a crowded courtroom?

She was glad he had made everyone else stay in the waiting room: Danielle; her dad, Nick; and even Jaydra, who now accompanied Cheyenne every time she left the house.

Jaydra, her bodyguard. Her keeper. Her dad said it was just until attention died down. What if someone else got it into their head to kidnap her, knowing he had already paid a million for her once?

"And keep your hands away from your mouth," Mr. Bennett said. "You need to speak clearly. The juror farthest from you should be able to hear every syllable."

Cheyenne started to nod, then caught herself. "Yes. Okay."

"And be sure not to chew gum." He hesitated. "Although, hmm, it could make you look younger. Let me think about it."

She straightened up. "Why would I want to look younger?" Because she was only five foot two, Cheyenne always sat and stood tall. She wore makeup, knowing it made her look older.

"We want the jury's sympathy." His voice firmed. "Ask your mom to pick out something that makes you look younger. Maybe something pink or with ruffles. "

Cheyenne didn't bother telling him she didn't own anything like that. Or that Danielle was her stepmom and certainly didn't pick out her clothes. She had already figured out this was a one-way conversation. Mr. Bennett wanted the jury to look at her and think she was helpless. Incapable. That she was a victim.

She hated that word.

"It's a fine line," he continued. "We want the jury to feel for you, but we also want them to trust every word you say. Initially, I'm going to take you through what happened, step by step. How you were kidnapped, how you escaped. I want them to feel the same things you did those three days. The terror of your kidnapping, the bravery of your escape."

Cheyenne hadn't felt brave, though. She shivered at the memory of running through the woods at night. Branches clawing her face. Tree roots tripping her up. Then it started to snow, adding the horrible knowledge that she must be leaving behind footprints.

"When it's the opposing counsel's turn to cross-examine you, he might ask if we've met before. It's fine to say yes. Just say I told you to tell the truth. If you tell the truth and tell it accurately, Wheeler can't cross you up. Never guess or make up an answer. If you don't know or don't remember, just say that. Answer only the exact question and then stop. For example, if I asked you how old you are, you would just say sixteen. You wouldn't tell me the time of day you were born or the name of the hospital. Don't volunteer anything."

"Okay." Cheyenne wanted to correct him, to say she would turn seventeen the day before the trial started, but Mr. Bennett didn't like interruptions. Her stomach felt queasy. What if she messed something up? What if Roy walked free? She remembered how he had howled her name as he did his best to kill her.

"That's another thing we might as well start practicing. Say 'yes, sir,' and 'no, sir,' to me and to Mr. Wheeler.

If you speak to the judge, say 'Your Honor.' And no joking around or getting agitated, even if you're feeling nervous. I'm not just talking about when you're on the stand. You need to keep it together at all times, even if you have an unexpected interaction in the hallway or outside the courthouse. Your behavior could be observed and factored into the jury's decision."

Interaction in the hallway. "Are you saying I might run into Griffin?" Her stomach twisted again. She pressed her fingers to her lips.

He touched her shoulder. The surprise of it, coming out of nowhere like that, made her jerk back.

"You don't need to worry. We'll make sure he never gets anywhere near you. And you've got Ms. Hamilton to protect you, of course." He meant Jaydra.

"Have you talked to him? To Griffin?" Cheyenne managed to sound like she didn't care.

"Yes. He's in town now. We've met several times to discuss his testimony."

Her heart sped up.

"He's the one who really has to worry, not you. Wheeler's going to focus on him like a laser. He'll try to get under his skin, make him lash out. He'll argue Griffin's the one who kidnapped you. Not his father."

"But it was an accident." Cheyenne didn't know who had been more surprised when each of them figured out the other was in the car. "Griffin was just trying to steal the Escalade, not me. He saw Danielle's keys, but he didn't notice me because I was lying down in the back. And he was going to let me go. It was his father's idea to ask for the money."

Mr. Bennett made a humming noise. "We only have Griffin's word for what he would have done. James Hixon is dead, and Thomas Meadors is in a mental hospital. And even though Griffin freely admitted stealing the car, I'm sure Wheeler's going to make a big deal about his plea bargain. He'll probably claim Griffin is lying about his father's involvement in exchange for not being sent to prison as an adult." He sighed. "Wheeler's going to eat him alive on cross."

Cheyenne must have made some small sound of protest because Mr. Bennett added, "I doubt he's going to ask much of you, since the jury will see you sympathetically. The one thing he might focus on is whether you're really capable of identifying Roy as the man who told your father to pay him five million dollars or else he would send you back in pieces. He's going to say it's impossible to identify someone by only voice or scent."

"I'm blind," Cheyenne said, "not stupid. Sir."

CHAPTER 2

PLAN B

ROY

If it weren't for Cheyenne Wilder, Roy Sawyer wouldn't have been lying on the top bunk in a Multnomah County Jail cell. A cell the size of a bathroom, which he shared with a guy named Tiny. Who obviously wasn't.

Twenty-one minutes before lights-on, Roy lay curled under a blanket the color and softness of a burlap sack, trying to ignore Tiny's snores. Tap-tap-tapping on a phone. It was a smartphone that could go online, but Roy was even smarter. First was the fact he had a phone at all. He had sweet-talked it out of the new nurse, Alice, who had taken a fancy to him.

Second, Roy never actually sent any e-mails on it, even though he and his half brother shared an account. *Is everything ready?* He saved the message in the drafts folder and waited for Dwayne to read it. Once he did, Dwayne would hit the delete key.

Poof! Roy's words would be gone. Leaving no record of what had been said. What had been planned.

Then Dwayne would write his own message and save it as a draft. Which Roy would then read and delete. And so on, back and forth. A whole conversation in invisible ink.

While Roy waited for Dwayne's reply, he watched the spider on the ceiling two feet above him busily tending her web. She had set up shop a week earlier, and since then she had provided him with hours of entertainment. The spider was the first nonhuman living thing he had seen in six months.

At home, he worked outside stripping stolen cars, or in a barn with the doors standing open. Hawks wheeled overhead. At night, coyotes yipped in the woods. When Roy was arrested, it had been winter. Now everything would be in bloom, bursting with life. He was still stuck in here.

Roy checked the time. Nineteen minutes left. Just before lights-on, he would slip the phone inside a sock and tuck it in his briefs. He worked on the jail's laundry crew, so he made sure he always got the baggiest pants.

Alice had also gotten him a charger, but there were no electrical outlets inside cells. The dayroom had outlets, but it was far too open. However, the laundry room had several that could be hidden behind stacks of neatly folded uniforms.

In a few minutes, he would roll out of his bunk, pull on blue scrubs over the pink-dyed T-shirt and briefs he was already wearing. Yank on pink tube socks and stuff his feet into plastic shower shoes. The end result was that he looked more or less like everyone else. But even prison couldn't take away his tattoos. An eagle. A snake. Satan riding a Harley. Barbed wire around a heart on his biceps that also read Janie in flowing script. This one had caught Alice's eye. She thought it was romantic.

He even had a spider tattoo, but it was of a tarantula, not a house spider like the one above his head. His spider had delicate striped legs and a fat brown belly speckled with black.

The bunk groaned as Tiny rolled over. The jail held more than five hundred people—snoring, farting, mumbling, and bickering. For most, it was catch and release. Others, like Roy, were awaiting trial. Afterward, he would go to state prison, a place he had resolved never to go. When he got out, he would be an old man.

And what happened hadn't even been his fault. It was his boy, Griffin, who brought Cheyenne home. Roy didn't plan it. Didn't ask for it. But when the radio said this girl was the daughter of Nike's president, well, who wouldn't want a little something for her safe return? Like finding a lost cell phone and getting a reward for giving it back. He hadn't touched a hair on her head, Roy thought as he watched the spider delicately wrap up a tiny fly.

Don't miss out on **APRIL HENRY**'s
other award-winning thrillers and mysteries!

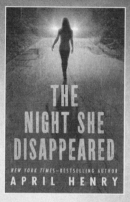

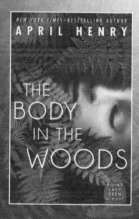